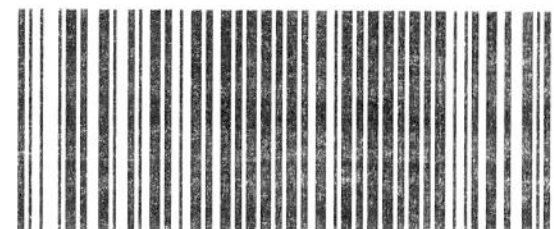

Also by Natasha D. Frazier

Devotionals

The Life Your Spirit Craves

Not Without You

Not Without You Prayer Journal

The Life Your Spirit Craves for Mommies

Pursuit

Fiction

Love, Lies & Consequences

Through Thick & Thin: Love, Lies & Consequences Book 2

Shattered Vows: Love, Lies & Consequences Book 3

Out of the Shadows: Love, Lies & Consequences Book 4

Kairos: The Perfect Time for Love

Fate (The Perfect Time for Love series)

With Every Breath (The McCall Family Series, book 1)

With Every Step (The McCall Family Series, book 2)

With Every Moment (The McCall Family Series, book 3)

Non-Fiction

How Long Are You Going to Wait?

Copyright © 2022 by Natasha D. Frazier
Published by Encouraging Works
Printed by Lightning Source, Inc.

ISBN: 978-0-9994496-8-4

Printed in the United States of America

All rights reserved. No portion of this book may be used in any form without the written permission of the publisher.

This is a work of fiction. Names, characters, businesses, places, events and incidents are either the products of the author's imagination or used in a fictitious manner. Any resemblance to actual persons, living or dead, or actual events is purely coincidental.

Editor: Chandra Sparks Splond

For autographed copies, please visit:
www.natashafrazier.com

Acknowledgements

This is a bit of a milestone year for me. November 2022 makes ten years since I've been a published author. And The Reunion is book 16! When I started in 2012, I wasn't sure where this journey would take me, but I've found it to be fulfilling and amazing. Some of my best days are when I meet my writing goals, along with everything else crammed into my day. So, my biggest thank you is to Jesus, who orders my steps, forgives my sins, and blesses me with the time and ability to do the thing I love – write.

My husband, Eddie, and my children Eden, Ethan, and Emilyn – thank you for your love, support, and selflessness. You often have to share me with fictional people and that isn't always ideal.

Chandra – Thank you for your editing expertise. This story wouldn't be as amazing without you.

Special thank you to my sister, Courtney, who gracefully endured my thousands of questions and text messages about what happens in jail. You rock! (She hasn't been to jail folks, she just worked in one for a while. Lol. Thought I'd clear that up.) Officer William Wade, thank you for giving me a well-rounded understanding of the arrest and investigative process. Officer Monalisa Harris, thank you for also being willing to answer my questions.

Page 35, you guys were there before the plot for this book fully came to fruition. Your feedback has blessed me throughout the development of this story. Thank you!

And the Dream Team, Thank you for reading and re-reading and listening to me go on and on about this story. We've talked about them like they're real people. Lol. Teamwork certainly makes the dream work. Thank you for being part of my team.

Dearest reader – Thank you for supporting me by reading, reviewing, and sharing my books with others. Keep it coming! I had you in mind as I typed every word. I'm excited to bring you something new with this romantic suspense series. I hope you enjoy it and I'm certainly on edge waiting to hear what you think.

Natasha

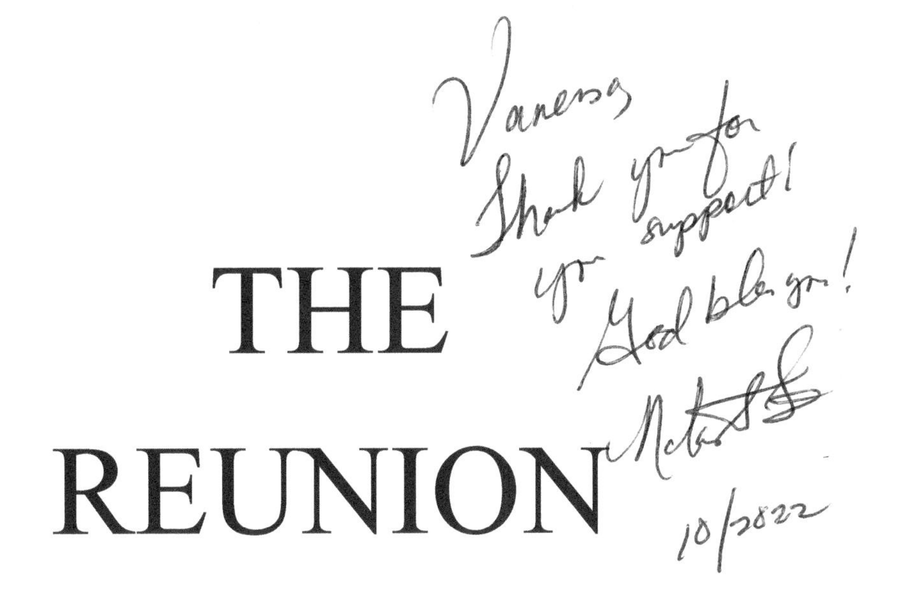

THE REUNION

Langston Sisters Series Book 1

One

Crystal Langston strolled into what had become her designated lane at Houston's The Lone Range. For the last seven months, Friday morning gun practice became a ritual. With her feet cemented in place, she rolled her shoulders, stretched her neck, slipped her protective gear over her eyes and the noise-cancelling headphones over her ears, and picked up the cool metal. It had become her companion. Gave her back her confidence. Put her in control.

And with the possibility of seeing her abusive ex-husband, NFL football star Dante Green, at tonight's twentieth college reunion from Houston University, she needed the practice. She had a busy day ahead with plans to attend a political fundraiser and the reunion, so she came in early.

She had to be prepared for anything.

Crystal relaxed her shoulders, lifted the gun, and aimed at her target. She fired round after round until she released all the pent-up anxiety she had about potentially seeing Dante again during the upcoming weekend. Going back to the place where they first met. Back to the place where she'd lost herself in him.

She pressed a button, and the target paper slid closer. Only one shot out of range. The rest of the bullets hit the head and chest area.

Yeah, she'd be prepared for Dante this go-round.

Satisfied with her session, Crystal packed away her gun, removed her eyewear and headphones, and joined the owner at the checkout area.

"Uncle Jeremy, thanks again for allowing me to come in early. I owe you."

The gray-haired longtime friend of her father smiled. "You're alright, young lady. You're like family. Besides, I'll just charge it to your old man. He can sponsor my next round of golf."

Crystal chuckled. "I'll give him a heads-up. See you next Friday at my regular time."

"Already got ya locked in. Take care."

Crystal squeezed his neck. "You can count on it."

∞

Around noon, Crystal sat among a crowd of donors to support her childhood best friend, Marcel Singleton, at his kickoff fundraising event for Harris County district attorney. Some of the attendees she recognized from Houston University's alumni association and others as well-known businessmen in the Houston, Texas area.

Normally, political events weren't her thing, but when she received the invitation, Crystal couldn't turn him down. She'd practically known him all her life, and it was probably time they reconnected. She attended as his friend, and in her capacity as chief executive officer of Langston Brands, a luxury handbag company launched by her great-grandparents more than seventy years ago.

The light chatter and soft music humming through the speakers ceased when Marcel appeared front and center in the room. He adjusted his tie and rested his hands on either side of the podium.

"I am proud to stand before you today and announce my candidacy for Harris County district attorney. Thank you for your generous donations and your faith in my abilities. I'm running for office because I want to see a criminal justice system that is fair, regardless of race, gender, and class. I want a community that is safe for the current and next generation. I want a criminal justice system that focuses on solving serious crimes that harm our communities, like murders and sexual assaults. And dear to my heart, I want a criminal justice system that is fair to the young black men who are seldom given a chance."

The room erupted into applause.

When had he become so handsome and mature?

Crystal missed the next part of his speech, captivated by the man Marcel had grown up to become. The man standing in front of the room was not the Marcel she remembered. Skinny, lanky, living life by the seat of his pants, and all about having fun. Not the Marcel holding the attention of everyone in the room. This Marcel was handsome, compassionate, and stirred something within her—like wanting to press her lips against his and find shelter in his strong arms kind of stir. His navy tailored suit didn't hide the muscles bulging beneath the sleeves. That thought felt wrong.

So wrong.

They'd been friends for thirty years.

That's it.

Marcel had always been the one guy in her life that she could call a faithful friend. He never made a move on her, so it was difficult to see him as anything but a friend.

Until now.

Crystal rubbed her collarbone like that would take away the thoughts that ran across her mind.

Marcel left the podium and strolled from table to table, thanking his donors. Her table was last, and she was the last person he addressed. When he spoke to her, Crystal's breath caught. She swallowed back the strange feelings and smiled. Instead of shaking her hand like he'd done to everyone else at her table, he wrapped his arms around her.

And it felt just as good as she imagined moments ago.

Stop.

He released her, but held her hands for a few seconds before letting go. "I'm so glad you could make it. It's been a while."

"I wouldn't miss it for anything. Are you planning to go to the reunion mixer tonight?"

He smiled and looked around before answering. "Will you be there?"

"Yes. I booked a room in Conroe. It's more convenient than taking that hour drive back to Katy in the middle of the night."

Marcel smiled with his bottom lip between his teeth. "I suppose I'll show my face for a few minutes."

"Well, I guess I'll see you there."

"How about we do more than just see each other? Let's find some time to talk."

Crystal took a deep breath. On the surface, that was an easy ask, but considering the weirdness happening in her heart and thoughts about him, she should make up an excuse, but instead she said, "Okay, sure. Come find me."

He squeezed her arm. "I've never lost you."

What is that supposed to mean?

Crystal strutted out of the building to her car. She needed to get out of Marcel's presence before she said or did something to twist the dynamics of their friendship. She'd known him almost her whole life, and being in his presence this afternoon was different—the kind of different she shouldn't even think about exploring.

∞

Marcel could have kicked himself for using that lame line, no matter how true it may be. Crystal Langston Green, in the flesh, though she dropped Green from her name when she and Dante divorced. She wore her hair long and straight with bangs as opposed to the curly chin-length style he'd become accustomed to seeing in online news articles. Her hairstyle was the only thing different about her since college. Time had been good to her. If she could go back twenty years and see herself today, she'd be pleased. Her beauty still illuminated the room. Of all the women he liked back then, Crystal was one he didn't have the guts to step to—they'd been friends since elementary.

Something about asking her out always felt like a line he shouldn't cross.

But this afternoon made him rethink every excuse he ever came up with to prevent him from taking the chance. For the brief moment she was in his arms, it felt different than before.

It felt right.

Olivia Singleton, his sister and campaign manager, slid next to him, bumped his shoulder with her own, and pulled him out of his Crystal trance. Her stats spoke for themselves. Every candidate's campaign she managed won their respective elections, so Marcel didn't mind the hefty price tag that came with her expertise. And although she was his sister, they agreed he'd pay her fee as if he was anyone else.

"I see she still has your heart on a string."

"Don't even go there. Crys is a friend to both of us."

"I'm pretty sure she and I aren't friends in the same way you two are. What's up with her?"

"We didn't get a chance to talk much. Hopefully, we can catch up at the reunion mixer tonight."

Olivia folded her arms across her chest. "You mean the mixer you said you weren't attending because you wanted to work on your speech for Texas Southern's townhall you're speaking at on Monday?"

Marcel shrugged. "Changed my mind."

"I bet. Anyway, take your head out of the clouds for a few minutes and go talk to Mr. Chavez. He and his partner like what you had to say up there tonight. He even mentioned hosting a fundraising event in your honor."

"I'm on it, boss."

Marcel left her side and strolled across the room, stopping along the way to speak to donors who were still lingering around. Mr. Chavez engulfed Marcel's hand in a two-hand hearty shake.

The tall, stout man wore a huge smile.

"Attorney, I have to say that your vision is one that we need to see come to fruition in our communities. When I heard the news about you running for DA from my partner, I told him we had to back you. DA Sanbridge has been in office too long, and if you ask me, he isn't doing a thing to improve our justice system."

Before Marcel decided to run for office, he'd made an oath with himself that he'd only discuss facts, not his opponent or other people. His goal was to run a clean and fair race.

"I appreciate your support, Mr. Chavez. Are there any questions I can answer for you?"

"I heard what you said up there about ensuring a fair criminal justice system, but what does that look like? What ideas do you have to implement that?"

Apparently, that had been a question on other people's minds, too, because a group of about ten formed a semicircle around him to hear his response.

"We need accountability, and this isn't something I can do alone, so if and when elected, I'll form a transition committee comprised of law enforcement, legal experts, faith-based and community leaders, and those directly impacted by the office who will help re-imagine the office to deliver justice for all. Together, we can make the office a leader on reform."

Mr. Chavez nodded with a facial expression that told Marcel he was impressed. He shook Marcel's hand again. "You have my full support, young man. I'll be in touch."

Marcel hung around and talked about his vision until he, Olivia, and a couple of his campaign volunteers were the only ones left. She strutted over and embraced him.

"You were made for this. You know that. Good job tonight. Now go ahead and get out of here. I'll follow up with the numbers later."

"Sounds like a plan."

Marcel retreated toward the exit.

"Tell Crystal I said hi."

Marcel tossed a hand in the air. Sure enough, Crystal was the only person on his mind. He wouldn't care if she was the only person who showed up at the reunion because she was the one person he couldn't wait to see again.

∞

Since Houston University was an hour's drive from her house in Katy, TX, Crystal booked a hotel room for the night in Conroe, TX. Once checked in, showered, and changed for the mixer, she stood before the wall mirror in her hotel and ran her hands along the length of her sheath dress. She'd done so for the sixth time, wearing down the carpet in the place she stood for the past ten minutes, half-listening to her sister through an earbud.

"Are you sure it's a good idea for you to go to this reunion? What if Dante is there?"

"I think it's about time I see him again and show my face to everyone else. Not wise for the world to believe he got the best of me."

Layla huffed. "Honestly, your attention should be focused on a successful launch of Langston Brands' new handbag collection, not on proving anyone right or wrong. You don't owe them anything, and I just don't have a good feeling about this. You know when I get these feelings in the pit of my belly, they're a sign of bad things to come. Just like—"

"I'm well aware of my obligations to our family's business. I've got that under control."

The primary reason Crystal attended business school at Houston University was to one day run her family's business. Her ambitions had finally come to fruition, so there was no way she'd allow Dante to mess that up for her again.

"My attendance at this reunion won't interfere with my job, and please don't even think about bringing up your premonitions about Dante. I've learned my lesson, and that's part of why I need to be here. You can understand that, right?"

The line went silent for a few seconds before Layla answered. "Not really. And Ava would agree with me, too."

Crystal could imagine the pout framing Layla's mouth. She shook her head. Their middle sister, Ava, always sided with Layla when they were being overprotective. At forty-one years old, Crystal was the oldest of the three, with Ava being eighteen months younger, and Layla eighteen months younger than Ava. Often, the trio was inseparable, but Crystal could appreciate the breathing room when she made decisions they didn't agree with.

"Sis, if it makes you feel any better, I'll be out of here tomorrow. I won't even be around to attend church services with the group on Sunday. Not too much can go wrong in a day, can it?"

Who was she kidding? Her entire life had changed in a day when Dante physically abused her. She fingered the scar above her right eyebrow, a permanent reminder of when he knocked her to the floor, and she bumped her head against the kitchen island on the way down. Crystal now wore bangs to hide the mark.

"Will you at least video call me tonight when you get back to your room so I know you're safe?"

"I thought I was the big sister."

"Yeah, but even big sisters need someone to look after them from time to time."

Crystal despised the references to her past, which further proved her point—she had to come to this reunion.

"Alright. Call you in a few hours."

Crystal tapped the earbud to end the call, scooped her phone from the counter, and opened the Facebook app to read over tonight's class reunion details again for the hundredth time. She tugged on the V-neck opening of her dress to allow the air to cool her warm skin. The saliva sliding down her throat did nothing to cure the dryness. Did her college classmates even care about what happened between her and Dante after all this time? The media couldn't keep her name out of their headlines, so she'd bet the same was true for them, too. Whatever the case, she'd set the record straight this weekend and move on with her life.

She glided toward the door, but turned to look at her half-opened suitcase sitting on the bed. One thing being with Dante taught her was she needed to always protect herself, yet she was halfway out the door without protection. No one would ever hurt her like he did, if she could help it. She sauntered over to the suitcase, opened the jewelry box–sized case, ran her hands over the cool metal, but hesitated before picking it up.

What am I doing? He won't hurt me in a room full of people.

She shut the case, shoved it under her garments, and rushed out of the room. On the other side of the door, she froze. Memories of the fear and helplessness slicing through her when Dante's towering presence punched her and sent her skidding across their oversized kitchen, and broke her nose, paralyzed her. Crystal caught the door before it closed and slipped back into the room. She reached into the suitcase once more and retrieved her protection.

Better safe than sorry.

Two

Crystal stepped out of her luxury coupe into the crisp evening air. Scarlet and royal blue balloons, coupled with the welcome sign, danced in the wind. She tightened her shawl around her arm and shuffled to the entrance of Houston University's multipurpose building. Back in undergrad, she attended sorority mixers, student government association meetings, and even a few dances inside the building. She smiled at the passing memories.

"I'd recognize that shape anywhere."

And she knew that voice anywhere—the voice of her nightmares. Crystal nearly jumped out of her skin and covered her mouth to suppress her squeal. She stiffened like a statue. Dante's breath on her skin caused the tiny hairs on her arms to stand at attention while snakelike slithers coursed through her veins. He still wore the same expensive cologne – an overpowering scent that made her stomach weave into knots and bile rise in her throat. Crystal pressed a hand to her throat and swallowed her disgust.

With his excessively high-priced watch clinging to his wrist, Dante reached around her frame, and opened the door. He extended his free hand. "After you."

Crystal forced a polite smile—so forced her cheeks hurt from the fakeness. "Thanks, but you can go on inside without me."

She sidestepped so he could show himself in. The last thing she wanted was a media blitz about how they showed up together or her pining behind him even after the way he physically abused her. The nightmare of seeing photos of her bruised face leaked to the media still haunted her. The nurse who took the photos was fired, but that didn't wipe away Crystal's embarrassment. No, she wanted no parts of whatever show he planned to put on for tonight's crowd.

The soft October breeze blew in concurrence, but Dante didn't budge. He released the door and stepped closer. Crystal stepped backward, nearly tripping in her heels, not realizing her legs trembled because of his presence. She clutched her handbag, her protection giving her some sense of confidence.

Dante must have smelled her fear because his gaze softened. That animalistic prowl-like glare in his eyes disappeared. "You're still afraid of me. How many times do I need to apologize for my mistakes?"

Crystal jutted her chin and stared him in the eyes. “Zero. It’s in the past, Dante.”

“Good. Now, can we please just have a nice weekend? Maybe this reunion—being back in the place we met—is what you need to be reminded of all the good times we had together, and maybe you’ll come to your senses and come home.”

“Dante, it’s been over a year since our divorce. I’m sure you know by now that isn’t going to happen. Besides, weren’t you just posted up with another woman on the cover of *People* magazine?”

He shrugged, and that smirk that made her skin crawl reappeared. “Never mind her. Surely you aren’t happy working with your family in some handbag business. I’m announcing my retirement this year. I could give you the money to start your own business, and you won’t have to be your family’s puppet. You know I can give you the life you want. Why are you making life hard on yourself?”

“See, that’s where you’re wrong.” Crystal took one step toward him, squeezing her clutch. Her knuckles ached because of it. “Any man putting his hands on me is not part of the life I want for myself. You should’ve thought about that before you lost your mind.” She lifted her bang to reveal the scar above her eyebrow. Something changed in his eyes, but she didn’t care.

A group of about ten of their classmates approached, including Dante's agent, Jacob Jackson, and the woman she'd seen in pictures with Dante.

Dante yanked open the door and gestured for her to enter. "I won't apologize again, but you'll soon come running back."

This time, Crystal walked inside. Over her shoulder, her voice echoed throughout the corridor, "Over my dead body—or maybe to bury yours."

She could have kept those last sentiments to herself, but it surely felt good to release it. There was a teeny-tiny part of her that would like to see Dante suffer, though she didn't have the guts for it to be by her hands.

Crystal scurried ahead to the check-in table, signed in, retrieved her name tag, and went in search of her sorority sisters. Thankful Dante engaged the group approaching them at the door, she could disappear and hopefully avoid him for the rest of the weekend.

Her mood lightened when she found her sorority sisters. After a round of hugs and compliments, her eyes locked on Marcel Singleton. He was making his rounds from table to table, just as he did at his political campaign launch earlier that afternoon. They'd been friends since elementary school, but had lost touch after college. Seeing him talk about his desire for justice and a fair criminal justice system made her see him as more than the guy she grew up with who liked every girl who passed his way, but as a man who'd matured with compassion for others. And it didn't hurt that he'd grown into a handsome man—a man who made her heart do crazy things when he stood before his donors and gave his speech.

Her thoughts trailed back to their earlier conversation. Marcel wanted to talk. They hadn't held a real conversation since college. Given they were once close, she should be looking forward to it, but instead, her fingertips grew cold, and it seemed someone put a squeeze on her lungs at the thought of their impending encounter.

∞

Thirty minutes into the mixer at his twenty-year college reunion and all Marcel Singleton could focus on was his DA campaign and spending time with Crystal. He made his rounds from table to table and then to recognizable faces huddled in their own private groups.

His recycled responses about his career and relationship status had already gotten old.

For those he cared to know anything about, he followed them on social media. And he'd returned to Houston University's homecoming every other year, so it wasn't like he'd miss anything by not attending the reunion mixer. If anything, his time might be better spent talking to donors about his political campaign.

"Hotshot!"

Marcel whipped his head around when he heard the nickname he'd earned on the basketball court.

"Hey, man. What's up?" Marcel grabbed and shook Anthony Brown's hand, then pulled him into a one-armed hug.

"I'm surprised to see you showed your face tonight. Figured with you being a hotshot criminal lawyer, you wouldn't have time for us little people."

Marcel chuckled and slapped Anthony's shoulder. "I could say the same about you. What are you up to these days?"

Anthony was one who didn't post much on social media. He was that friend who usually popped up to thank everyone for birthday wishes and disappeared for another year.

"Still working in public accounting, man. Teresa started her make-up business, so aside from the day job, I'm her accountant."

"That's cool, man. Good for her. Is she here?"

Anthony pointed. "Yeah. She's over there talking to her sorority sisters."

Marcel's attention shifted to the woman standing next to Anthony's wife: Crystal.

He hadn't been able to stop thinking about her since their encounter, and quite frankly, she'd been the driving force behind his decision to attend tonight's mixer.

"I'm gonna assume you're gawking at one of Teresa's sorors. I don't wanna have to handle you in here."

Marcel chuckled and nodded in Crystal's direction. In as casual a voice as he could muster, he said, "Teresa keep in touch with Crystal?"

"Don't go there, man. I know you two were friends and all, but you know she has Dante issues. I'd hate for you to get caught up in that."

"Reel it back in. Everyone knows about her and Dante. Just wondering how she's doing. That's all."

When had he stooped to the level of hustling up information about her through third parties?

"Go see for yourself, my brother."

Marcel parted his lips to respond, but the DJ jumped on the mic and introduced Dante when he entered the room, causing an uproar from the crowd loud enough to drown out anything he would have said. Instead of focusing on Dante, Marcel's attention shifted back to Crystal. The smile that graced her face moments ago was gone. Marcel tore his gaze away from Crystal to check his vibrating phone. His sister and campaign manager, Olivia, had sent him a text message:

O: We've raised $500k this afternoon!

M: Thanks for the update, Liv. Pretty good for the first fundraiser, right?

O: I think so, but we still have a long way to go. Enjoy your evening, and we'll talk later.

That tidbit of good news put his mind at ease for the evening.

Marcel tucked his phone away, and despite Anthony's warning, he shuffled through the crowd and tables and made his way to Crystal's side. At one point, they'd been close friends. As a lawyer, he was trained to be a quick thinker, but when he got close to her, all he could muster was, "Hi," which didn't seem to be enough after not talking to her since college, and certainly not enough after how she felt in his arms when he hugged her at his fundraiser a few hours ago.

Her features softened, and she gave a smile that made him feel like he'd won the lottery.

"Hey, Marcel. Congrats again on throwing your hat in the race for DA. I'm proud of you."

"Thanks. It's a little unfair that you know things about me and I don't know much about what's happening with you."

Crystal averted her eyes and sipped her drink. "I think you and everyone else here knows enough about me. You running for DA is bigger than anything happening in my life right now." She leaned in and bumped his shoulder with hers.

"Maybe I can get you to work on my campaign."

"I can support, but I don't know about any grassroots work. Being the new CEO of Langston Brands has my hands full."

"I'm happy to see you're holding up well after everything that went down with Dante. Sorry you had to go through that."

Her eyes widened like she was surprised he mentioned Dante's name. A mix of horror and something else flashed in her eyes, then her gaze traveled away from him, and he followed. Dante glared at them, like he had rights to Crystal and Marcel infringed upon them. Marcel returned his glare, almost daring him to make a move. He hadn't been there to stop Dante from hurting her before, but there was no way he'd allow the man to touch Crystal again.

Dante's agent whispered something in his ear, and he averted his gaze away from Marcel. Marcel looked back at Crystal. Her nose flared, and her eyes tightened.

"Yeah, me, too. Mind if we go outside to talk? It's a little loud in here."

Marcel picked up on the cue and followed Crystal out of the room. They sat on a bench in the hallway. The throwback music and chattering voices could still be heard, but at least now they could hear more of each other.

"If I'm overstepping, let me know, but I have to ask: Are you okay? Is Dante threatening you or something? I can't help but notice that you look at him like you're afraid or like you're minutes from taking him out."

Crystal pulled her wrap around her shoulders and stared ahead. "No. He's not threatening me. And honestly, I'd love the chance to pay him back for the hurt he's caused me, both publicly and privately, but I'm okay. I'll never let him hurt me again. I'd kill him first."

Marcel didn't have any doubt she meant every word. He suppressed a shudder at the iciness that laced her voice and reached out to squeeze her hand.

"I hate you had to go through that." *I never would have done that to you.*

"Yeah, me, too, but it's over now. I've severed ties with him. It's just that seeing him tonight brings back a lot of anger and resentment I thought I'd let go—or at least hoped I did."

"But you didn't." Marcel shifted to face her. "It's okay to be angry because of what happened, as long as you don't allow it to control you."

Crystal turned to face him. She pursed her lips and squinted her eyes. They held a faraway look. He was sure her memories haunted her. "It's been more than a year since our divorce, and I still can't believe he abused me. The man who was supposed to love and cherish me hit me like I was a player on the football field."

Tears filled her eyes, and Marcel thought that would be his undoing. This time, he wrapped his arm around her shoulder and kissed the top of her head. *Please don't cry.* "I'm so sorry."

"Thanks, Marcel. It isn't your fault. It's his, and he'll get what's coming to him."

Three

Crystal bit her tongue. The last thing she wanted Marcel or anyone else to believe was that she was a scorned, bitter woman with her heart set on revenge. She and Marcel went way back, though—friends since fourth grade. If anyone understood what she was going through, it was him. He'd always been that one friend she could count on when going through tough times, yet she didn't dare reach out to him when she had her issues with Dante.

She inhaled and released a slow, calming breath. "Let's not dwell on my troubles, though. Tell me what you've been up to. It's been a long while since we've talked."

Crystal leaned in and gave his knee a soft push. He looked at her like she'd grown another head, but then gave the kind of smile that assured her he was okay. Marcel shifted so he completely faced her.

"It has. But you know that isn't my fault. You were a married woman. Besides, Dante never liked the idea of us being friends, no matter how long we've known each other."

"Yeah. He was a little on the jealous side."

Marcel chuckled. "A little is putting it a little too nicely. I almost flunked out of college because of him. Made me lose my study partner."

Crystal snorted. "You need to stop."

"I'm serious. I missed hanging out with you."

"Dude, cut it out. You dated half the campus."

Marcel threw his head back and laughed harder. "Doesn't mean I couldn't still miss you. What else was I supposed to do? I had to find a way to get over losing you."

The way his voice deepened and eyes gazed into hers almost gave her an arrhythmia. Had Marcel always liked her and she somehow missed all the signs? Crystal gnawed on her bottom lip. Her thoughts trailed back to yesteryears when she and Marcel spent more than enough time together. Some would say too much time together considering they weren't dating. Because of all the time they spent with each other in college, they'd both been the reason relationships with other people didn't work.

Until Dante.

Because of him, her friendship with Marcel was never the same.

"Crys, can we talk?" Dante's voice cut through her thoughts when he walked into the hallway, invading her space. Though the area was large enough for their entire class, the mere fact she and Dante occupied the same area brought an onset of claustrophobia.

Marcel jumped up like he was prepared to defend her honor, but she didn't need anyone's protection, though when he'd initiated their conversation inside the mixer area, that was the first moment she'd relaxed since she'd arrived.

Crystal stood and folded her arms across her chest. "What is there for us to talk about, Dante?"

Dante didn't address her at first. He turned his attention to Marcel. "Look, bro, let the air out of your chest. I need to talk to my wife."

"Ex-wife. Don't come out here making a scene. What do you want?"

Dante lifted his palms in surrender. "Crys, can we please talk in private? It won't take long."

Crystal looked to Marcel. He didn't speak, but raised an eyebrow as if to question whether she needed him to step in for her. Maybe send Dante packing for good since he wouldn't listen to her. Somehow the threats from her father seemed to have faded to the back of Dante's mind. She released a pent-up sigh and relaxed her shoulders.

Against the small voice in her head whisper-shouting for her to stay put, she said, "Okay, but only five minutes."

She touched Marcel's arm. "I'll be right back. If I'm not back in seven minutes, you have my permission to search for me."

Marcel whipped his phone from his pocket and hit the side key to check the time. "Deal."

With each step, her stomach twisted into tiny knots. Her mind screamed, *You know better.* Her heart hammered in her chest. She could feel Marcel's eyes burning a hole in the back of her head with the increasing distance she put between them. Dante led her around the corner, farther down the hall where the walls were void of everything but old paint. The music and voices became fainter. She kept about a six-foot distance between the two of them so if he made any threatening movement, she had time to pull her gun.

He stopped at the end of the hall and turned to face her. She took two steps back.

"Why are you acting like you're afraid of me? What happened to the woman who vowed to love me till death do us part?"

Crystal threw her head back and laughed, then looked over her shoulder. "Are you kidding me right now? Where are the cameras?"

Dante reached for her hands, but Crystal snatched away and took three steps back. *Why am I even entertaining this fool?* "Don't touch me. What do you want to talk about?"

"You know you're the only reason I showed up this weekend, right?"

"I don't care why you're here. Our divorce has been final for over a year, and to answer your question, the woman who vowed to love you till death do us part almost died in the hospital after you nearly beat her to death. I'll never give you the chance to do that to me again, so for the final time, good-bye, and have a nice life."

Dante grabbed her arm a little too hard, and Crystal flashed back to that day she'd tried hard to forget—the second and final time he'd physically abused her. He'd come home after losing a game and taken all his frustrations out on her face. Before she left the hospital, photos of her bruised face were circulating entertainment media, thanks to a nurse looking for a quick buck.

She believed his rage stemmed from more than him reeling from losing a football game, but she never stuck around to find out.

It didn't matter. All that mattered was her life.

But today, she wouldn't allow him to hurt her. She turned and thrust her foot in his groin as hard as she could. He shouted an expletive, grabbed himself and fell to his knees. Crystal almost twisted her ankle getting away from him. Her hands and legs shook while she ran back to Marcel.

After what seemed like an eternity, she crashed into his arms.

"Is everything okay? You're shaking." Marcel peered over her shoulder. "Where's Dante? Did he hurt you?"

Crystal shook her head and buried it deeper into his chest. The cedar wood scent emanating from his skin tantalized her senses. Calmed her. And made her want to snuggle closer in his embrace.

"No."

But she couldn't erase the scene with Dante out of her mind. Would he leave her alone or attempt to corner her again?

Four

The bright lights, upbeat party music, and smiling faces did nothing to curb the uneasiness snaking through Crystal's limbs. She'd caught Dante glancing in her direction a few times with that smirk on his face. He had to be up to something. She just hoped she could enjoy the rest of the evening without coming face-to-face with him again. The uncomfortable activity in the pit of her belly warned her to leave now.

But she had Marcel.

Hopefully, he'd stop her from doing anything crazy.

Hopefully, his presence would prevent Dante from doing anything crazy.

Marcel grazed the back of her hand. "You sure nothing happened with Dante?"

She jumped, nearly knocking over the glass of soda she'd been nursing. The ice cubes had melted.

Crystal took slow, even breaths.

"I'm okay. Dante didn't do anything to me, and I don't think he'll be bothering me anymore."

Next time I may not be so nice.

She parted her lips in a smile long enough for worry lines in Marcel's forehead to dissipate.

"Wanna dance with me?"

Crystal felt a more genuine smile form on her lips. It was something about the way he asked. Like he desired to be more than friends, but that was a silly thought. They'd always been friends—no romantic interest on either of their part. A small voice in the back of her mind screamed, *You know that's a lie.*

Could that be why Dante had always been uncomfortable with her and Marcel's friendship?

She shook her head to dismiss the thoughts.

"No?"

"Of course, I'll dance with you."

Marcel stood and held out his hand. She accepted it and followed him to the dance floor. The music transitioned to a slow song, and she hesitated.

"I still want my dance, no matter what song is playing."

Crystal chuckled, unsure about being so close to him for at least three-and-a-half minutes, especially after the way her body responded to being in his arms for a few seconds back at the fundraiser. Marcel must have sensed her uneasiness because he took her hands and placed them on his broad shoulders. His hands encircled her waist.

"Such a shame I had to wait this long for my dance."

Crystal bit back a smile.

"What do you mean, *wait this long*? You had plenty of opportunities to dance with me if I recall correctly. The seventh- and eighth-grade sweetheart dances. At least fifty dances in high school. Junior and senior prom. Should I go on and talk about your missed opportunities on this campus?"

Marcel tossed his head back, and a hearty laugh escaped his lips. "Nah. You've made your point. You lumped me into the friend zone early on. I didn't think you were interested."

Heat emanated from her skin. The way Marcel's eyes bore into hers told her he was interested—seriously. When had that happened? The thought made her uncomfortable and excited at the same time. A shiver coursed through her core. She averted her gaze and shifted her attention to everyone she could see to her right because she couldn't see over his shoulder.

"There's the look that made me keep my mouth shut all this time."

Crystal turned her attention back to Marcel and looked him the eyes. "I'm sorry. I guess I'm a bit surprised. I never got the vibe you were interested in anything other than friendship with me the way you played the field."

"Like I said earlier, I had to do something to get my mind off you."

If only he'd said something years ago—before she met Dante or even before she'd married Dante.

The song transitioned to something more upbeat, and Marcel excused himself to take a call. Crystal released a sigh of relief. This wasn't a conversation she'd ever thought she'd have with Marcel.

She reclaimed her seat. Instead of mingling with anyone else, she whipped out her phone to check e-mails. That would take her mind off whatever was happening with her and Marcel.

Crystal hadn't made it through the first e-mail when a group shuffled toward the stage. She glanced to see Dante climbing the steps. Of course, he drew everyone's attention. She refrained from rolling her eyes. Dante whispered into the DJ's ear, and the music quieted. His agent, Jacob Jackson, who went everywhere with him, handed him a microphone. Wynter, the woman she'd seen in recent photos with him, stood waiting center stage in a crimson form-fitting dress that sparkled under the lights. Anyone close enough could probably count her teeth, she smiled so wide. Her hands were clasped at her chest while she shifted from one heel-clad foot to the other, anxious for what was coming next. Crystal could only assume he was about to propose or even announce his engagement to her. She was dressed fancier than most women in attendance.

Hopefully, that meant he'd leave her alone for good.

She sipped her drink and waited.

"You all have been down with me from day one—since I got drafted right out of college— and I can't thank you enough for your support. Even through my roughest times, y'all stood by me."

His eyes locked on Crystal's. She squirmed in her seat. Her heart rate doubled. She sipped her drink, hoping the liquid would wash away her discomfort. It didn't. The diet soda rose back up into her throat, and she forced it back down.

"My man, Jacob Jackson, is the best agent in the business. And without him, I'm sure I wouldn't be where I am. Thanks, man." Dante slapped Jacob's back, following the sentiment with a one-armed hug.

"So tonight, I want to make a special announcement." He paused as if to ensure he had the attention of everyone in the room—and he did, along with phone cameras. Some classmates were even live streaming to social media. He scanned the expanse of the room until he locked eyes with Crystal's again.

Get on with it.

"I've loved every moment of the last twenty years playing pro ball, and since this is where it all started, this is where I'd like to officially announce that I'm retiring from the NFL."

Wynter's smile faded, and that shimmer left her eyes. She recovered and plastered on a smile that didn't reach her eyes.

Jacob's expression didn't falter. Instead, he exchanged a glance with Wynter and kept his position next to Dante like a bodyguard.

Murmurs and a round of applause filled the room until Dante lifted his hand to signal he wasn't finished. The crowd quieted.

"And…though we went through some difficult times, Houston University's favorite couple is getting back together."

Gasps and applause filled the room.

"That's right. You heard it here first. I'm retiring from the NFL, and I'm getting Crystal back. Wish me luck." Dante kissed two fingers and pushed them in the air.

Wynter's eyes grew as wide as saucers. Even from where Crystal sat about fifty feet from the stage, she could see the tears spring to the woman's eyes before she stormed off the stage. Jacob whispered in Dante's ear and took off after her. As his agent and friend, Jacob always cleaned up Dante's messes. Wynter scurrying off the stage in shame appeared to be one of them.

Blood rushed through Crystal's veins. Every nerve in her head pulsed. Her limbs shook.

It didn't take long for their classmates to spot her in the crowd. Camera phones were now pointing in her direction. She hopped off the stool, and what felt like a hundred needles stabbed the bottom of her feet. Even still, she didn't allow the ache to stop her from dashing out of the room to get away from Dante and all the cameras. She'd done her time in the entertainment news headlines. She was done.

Dante shouted, "Crys, wait."

Crystal didn't stop.

As if he was running a play on the football field, Dante maneuvered around her and grabbed her shoulders. Her skin stung from the interaction, made her stop in her tracks.

Crystal growled, "Get your hands off me, or I swear I'll kill you."

Several *oohs* erupted from behind her.

Crystal wrestled herself out of his grip and turned to see phones pointing in their direction.

She closed her eyes briefly and blew a slow stream of air. There was no way she would give these people more of a show than Dante had already given.

Dante addressed the crowd behind them. "Can we have some privacy?"

Not a soul budged.

Except Crystal.

She spun on her heel to get away from him. Again, he grabbed her shoulders and pulled her into a multipurpose room, shutting the door behind them, blocking her exit.

"Crys, please just hear me out."

"What kind of foolishness was that, Dante? Why would you do that to me? I've told you I want nothing else to do with you."

"But, baby, you know when I hurt you, I wasn't myself. I've apologized for that, and I've changed."

He grabbed her by the arm, and she could swear he had the same look in his eyes he had when he punched her in the jaw. She'd suffered a concussion, received a dental implant to replace the tooth he'd knocked out, and sported a permanent scar above her right eyebrow.

She wrestled out of his grasp, whipped the gun from her purse, and pointed it at him – aiming it the same way she learned at the gun range.

Dante reached toward her. "Crys, wait. What are you doing?"

"Probably what I should have done while you were treating me like I was your punching bag." She clicked the safety.

"Wait," Dante pleaded. "I know I've hurt you, and I'm sorry, but I know you. You don't have it in you to pull the trigger."

Crystal planted her feet firmer and flexed her hands around the Glock.

"You sure about that?"

Her heart hammered in her ears. Her hands trembled, but she committed to protecting herself. She wouldn't end up with a matching scar above her left eyebrow.

Crystal hissed through clenched teeth. “Don’t you move another inch, or the last thing you’ll feel is a round of bullets.”

“I’m sorry I ever hurt you. I don’t know what happened to me or what made me treat you the way I did. No matter what you may think, I still love you, and I’ll never hurt you again.”

His softened eyes reminded her of when they’d dated in college. Whatever happened to that man? She relaxed her shoulders and took a step back. For the first time, Crystal believed he regretted his actions, but his apology would never be enough to make her change her mind about being with him again.

She kept the gun pointed at him and backed farther away.

Crystal looked over her shoulder, hoping to spot another exit.

The room was a smaller multipurpose room with partitions to her left, right, and rear. The rear partition had a small opening with a cutout that looked like a door to exit. That’s how she’d get out of here and avoid the cameras. This whole evening had turned into one big disaster.

Crystal took another step back.

“I’m glad you’ve changed Dante, but I’ve made my decision. I want nothing else to do with you and refuse to give you the opportunity to hurt me again.” Crystal lifted her bangs to expose the scar above her brow. “You did this to me.”

Dante beat his chest, his voice raising with every word. "I apologized. I'm leaving the game. What else do you want from me?"

"I want you to stay out of my life and go back out there and tell everyone you lied. We're not getting back together, and I'm never coming back to you."

"And if I don't, are you planning to shoot me?"

Crystal cocked her head and raised one eyebrow. She flexed her sweaty hands around the metal, forcing them steady. Like a dog, Dante could smell fear, so she planted her feet, ground her teeth, and filled her chest with enough air to fill a balloon.

She kept the gun aimed at Dante and backed away toward the partition door she'd spotted moments ago, into an empty room.

Thankfully, Dante didn't move, but the look on his face told her that wasn't the last she'd hear from him. She closed the partition and retreated toward an exit that led to the side of the building.

Crystal pushed the door open, but her body numbed when she heard Dante shout, "No. Don't," and two gunshots rang through the air.

She glanced down at her trembling hand still holding her own gun, clicked the safety, and pushed it back into her purse.

Managing to pull herself of out her temporary trance, she powered through the door into the cool evening air and ran around to the front of the building. A myriad of thoughts plowed through her mind.

Was Dante shot?

If so, who did it?

Would people blame her?

Her legs were like putty, so she wasn't even sure how they carried her to the front of the building.

Commotion filled the area. Some people hurried back inside the building with their phones raised in the air to see and record what happened, something she'd never understand. Others rushed out of the building, talking over one another. But there was one distinctive statement she heard through the chatter.

"Crystal killed Dante," she heard someone shout.

Her body froze.

Her vision blurred.

Her ears plugged.

She was the last person seen with him.

Would anyone believe she didn't do it?

Five

Marcel ended his call with Olivia when he saw the crowd gathering in front of the building. He ran over to see if he could spot Crystal in the group. After five minutes of searching for her, they locked eyes, and Crystal ran and threw her shaky body in his arms.

Crystal trembled hard enough to put his senses on high alert. So he held her until she pulled away.

"You okay?"

Crystal's eyelids fluttered before tears pooled in her eyes.

She nodded. "I'm okay, but Dante is dead."

"What happened?"

Marcel braced himself for what she would say next. Dante's death wasn't good, but the growing ache in his body warned him that the situation was much worse. He squeezed her hands, encouraging her to continue.

"He made this announcement about retiring and us getting back together."

"What?"

She shook her head. "It's not true. At least not the part about us getting back together. After he stood in front of everyone and lied, I ran out of the room. He followed me."

Crystal answered his unasked question. She could see it in his eyes.

"It wasn't me. He pulled me into a room where we argued for a minute. I pulled a gun on him, but I didn't use it. I was halfway out the door when I heard the gunshots."

Marcel nodded. Relief coursed through him. "It'll be okay, then. I'm sure we'll find out what happened in no time with just about everybody here with video."

Panic flickered in her eyes.

"What's the matter?"

"I'm one hundred percent sure there's video of me going into the room alone with him. What if the cops think I did it?"

"You said you were out of there when you heard the shots. I'm sure there's video of that, too."

Crystal shook her head. Her voice was hoarse like she'd been screaming. "I didn't go out the same way I went in. I left through a partition that led to an empty room with an outside exit. No one saw me leave."

Marcel wiped his palm over his face, threw his head back, and exhaled.

He and Crystal both turned to see phones pointed in their direction, with accusations of Crystal being last seen with him alive.

"I heard her say she'd kill him," one classmate said.

Another classmate added, "Right. And then she's in the room with him and he wound up dead. That ain't no coincidence."

Marcel placed a hand on her back and ushered her away from the crowd.

The odds weren't in her favor.

"You're gonna need a lawyer. I'll represent you."

He wished he could take away the horror plastered over her face. Instead, he pulled her into his arms again. Things were likely going to get worse before they got better.

Sirens wailed in the distance, growing louder by the second. Most of their classmates now huddled in front of the school. Camera phones raised in the air. Hundreds of eyes gazed in their direction, with murmurs of Crystal killing Dante.

Paramedics rushed on the scene, police cruisers filling in behind them. Crystal's hand felt cold in his. He squeezed her hand for assurance while they watched the scene unfold.

More officers filled the parking lot, ushering everyone away from the building while others locked down the building and sealed the exits.

The flashing blue and white lights put the detective in the spotlight. "We need everyone back inside the facility where my fellow officers will take a written statement from each one of you. Please include your name and a good phone number in case we need to contact you after tonight. No one is to leave the premises until I give the order."

∞

The baldheaded man in charge with piercing hazel eyes and a neatly trimmed beard lowered his voice, and spoke to about eight officers standing near him. Crystal assumed he was the detective since he was the only one not in uniform but giving orders. If she didn't know any better, she'd think he'd already made up his mind that she was guilty. Maybe it was all in her head, but that tiny voice in her mind told her she was right this time. The way he squinted and twisted his lips gave him away. *Weren't officers were supposed to keep neutral expressions?*

Crystal glanced down at her hands to see that she'd been squeezing the life out of Marcel's fingers.

"I'm sorry. Didn't mean to hurt you."

"You didn't." He placed a gentle hand on her back and ushered her toward the building so they could give their statements.

But they didn't make it inside.

One of the officers, stopped them.

"Ma'am, please place your hands behind your back."

The officer cuffed her. The cold metal secured around her wrists ensured her that this wasn't a nightmare. Dante's murder was real and she was about to be arrested for a crime she didn't commit.

Her back burned from the accusing eyes of her classmates. All she could think about was who would've done such a thing. From all she knew, they were all Dante fans. Her eyes settled on his agent and long-time friend Jacob Jackson filing into the building. Thankfully, his eyes weren't laser beams because she'd be seared in half by now. His arms were wrapped around Wynter, who was screaming, crying, and pointing at Crystal saying, "Why would you do this to him?"

Her mind reeled back to her argument with Dante. Why didn't she just leave after her first run-in with him?

The police officer led her to the baldhead detective.

Marcel extended his hand toward the detective. "I'm Attorney Marcel Singleton and I'm representing Ms. Langston. Is she under arrest? If not, I respectfully ask that you remove the handcuffs. They aren't necessary."

The detective nodded toward the officer, who then removed the cuffs.

"Ms. Langston, I need you to come downtown to give your statement. Someone will return you to your vehicle."

Crystal nodded. "Okay."

"Attorney, you can meet your client downtown."

Marcel gave Crystal's arm a light squeeze. "Don't worry. I'll be right there."

The officer escorted her to the police cruiser. She followed with her chin up, though her insides were involved in a fight of their own. The officer opened the door and she slid into the dipped seat.

Trapped.

No door handles.

And a prisoner partition separating her from the officer in the driver's seat.

News station vans and photographers were now on the scene.

How can this be happening?

Inside the precinct, the officer led her into a room where she came face-to-face with Officer Baldhead Hazel Eyes. He stood and shook her hand. Marcel occupied the seat next to hers. He nodded.

"I'm Detective Elijah Diggins. Please have a seat."

She sat. Crystal hated the way his eyes pierced hers. He made her feel guilty even though she wasn't.

"You're Ms. Crystal Green, am I right?"

"It's Langston." She forced a smile. Should she be smiling considering the circumstances?

Detective Diggins nodded and scribbled on his notepad. He removed his jacket and folded the sleeves on his shirt, a move that suggested to Crystal he planned to be there for a while.

Why is he getting comfortable?

Beads of sweat rolled down her back.

Lord, I can't go to jail.

"Ms. Langston, as I understand it, you and the victim, Mr. Dante Green, are ex-spouses. Is that correct?"

"Yes."

"And how long have you two been divorced?"

"A little over a year." Though the last three years of her marriage were the equivalent to Satan's playground.

He scribbled on his notepad again.

"How would you describe your relationship with Mr. Green?"

"There is no relationship. We haven't communicated since the divorce."

He nodded, and she couldn't help but believe he already had his mind made up about her. She glanced at Marcel. His nod gave her some level of assurance.

"Okay then. Let's talk about tonight. Do you have any knowledge about what happened to him?"

She shook her head and did her best to keep her voice even. "No."

She prayed her facial expression was neutral. She maintained eye contact with Detective Diggins. Her body was so stiff in her seat that she could've easily been mistaken for a statue.

"Do you know anyone who might want to hurt him?"

"I do not."

"Where were you when the victim was shot?"

"Outside."

Not technically. Almost outside was more like it. It took less than a minute for him to get shot from the time she left him, but even she would think she was guilty if she offered that detail.

He held her gaze for a full ten seconds before shifting in his seat. He clasped and rested his hands on the wooden desk that was way past its time to be replaced. It creaked under his weight.

"Do you have any idea what happened to him? I've had several witnesses with video who attest to hearing you say you'd kill Mr. Green and that show you entering the room alone with him. He never left the room. No one saw you leave the room either. Now he's dead."

Crystal swallowed the rock in her throat and glanced toward Marcel. "I don't know what happened to him."

"Ms. Langston, I'm afraid you're under arrest for the murder of Mr. Dante Green."

Detective Diggins rose from his seat, rounded the desk, and stood in front of Crystal.

The handcuffs taunted her. "Please stand."

Marcel leaned toward her. "I know this looks bad, but I'm going to get you out of here. We both know you didn't do it. Just leave it to me to prove it."

Crystal wanted to believe Marcel, but right now, those were just words—words that didn't provide any comfort with her on the way to jail.

She followed the detective's instructions and stood. The back of her eyes stung with tears when the handcuffs closed around her wrists.

Six

Every step Crystal took through Montgomery County jail was like walking through drying cement. On top of that, the musty scent in the air assaulted her nostrils. She'd never smelled anything so horrible—a combination of vomit, pepper spray, mold, and armpits that hadn't been scrubbed in weeks. The urge to puke bounced around in her throat, and if she didn't know any better, she'd swear ants had somehow made their way along her skin and traveled like they were carrying food away from a barbecue picnic table back to their queen.

Detective Diggins escorted her to the booking window and handed her off to a female officer like she was some type of common criminal. The officer frisked her. Disgust trailed every touch. Crystal shivered. Dark thoughts surfaced. *Probably should've pulled the trigger.*

The female officer stripped her of jewelry and her leather crossbody purse. She searched Crystal's purse and removed the gun, placing it in an evidence bag. Crystal stood there with her head held high while the clerk assessed her clothes and typed the description in the computer. She was innocent. There was no reason for her to hang her head low.

"Any tattoos or birthmarks?" the clerk asked in a you-know-the-drill tone. Her red bob danced around her face with each turn of her head.

"None."

The clerk followed with questions regarding her eye color and hair color.

The female officer didn't say anything until it was time for them to take her mugshot.

Mugshot.

Never in her life did she think she'd ever get one of those. If anything, Dante belonged in the space where she stood. She'd never done anything to deserve a jail cell.

"Hold this and face forward."

Crystal took the placard with her name, birthday, weight, and booking ID written on it. She stepped in front of the mugshot height chart and turned to face the officer. The top of her head hardly reached the five-foot, three-inch line.

"Turn to the left."

A chill coursed through her body, though the station was warm and muggy. She turned to the left, then followed instructions for the right.

"Stretch your hands toward me, palms up. We're going to test you for gunshot residue."

The officer swabbed her palms, between the web of her fingers, and the back of her hands. She despised the fact they were treating her like a criminal. Sure, she pulled a gun on Dante, but no one could attest that she pulled the trigger. In fact, she hadn't fired her gun since earlier that morning at the gun range. They could dust, test, and do whatever else they wanted, but they weren't going to find her at fault in killing Dante.

The officer handed an orange jumpsuit and a pair of inmate shoes to Crystal, then escorted her into the restroom to change, where the awful scent was much worse.

I won't be wearing these long. C'mon, Marcel.

She slipped out of her dress and shoes and hung the dress over the stall door. Though the temperature was set to freezing, Crystal took advantage of every second she had left outside of that cell, inching her limbs into the jumpsuit.

The officer banged on the stall door.

"Time's up."

Her heart dropped to her belly, and she prayed. *Please, God, don't let me have to spend more than one night here. Help Marcel do whatever he needs to do to get me out of this place.* She zipped the suit, slipped into the pair of inmate shoes, stepped out of the stall, and handed her clothes to the officer, who placed them inside a plastic bag. Orange was one of her favorite colors, but that jumpsuit wasn't flattering in the least bit.

This can't be real.

She followed the officer to a cell labeled 5K1. The officer signaled toward the camera overhead, and the door slid open. Crystal took five heavy steps across the threshold, then the door shut behind her, locking her inside.

Claustrophobia set in. Crystal gripped her chest and heaved. The funky stench in the air cut the heaving short, though. The idea of sucking in the unpleasant air helped her get a grip.

Okay. This isn't forever. It's temporary. Marcel's got this.

The day's activity weighed on her, and all she wanted to do was rest. But again, the thought of resting her head on that makeshift bed, instead of her memory foam mattress, caused a shiver to run through her body. So, for as long as she could, she paced the tiny space. When she and Dante were married, their powder room was larger than the area she now occupied.

What if Marcel couldn't get her out of this?

The same officer passed through the area making rounds. Crystal rushed to the bars, squeezed, and yelled, "Hey, what about my phone call?"

Though dark, she could see the officer halt and turn around.

Why hadn't they offered her that call?

The officer signaled with her hand again, and the door slid open. The short and stout officer with an unbothered expression led her to a holding area.

She lifted the receiver, held her breath, and dialed her sister Layla.

"Crystal, are you okay? I've called you at least twenty times. Why haven't you been answering your phone? Dante's murder has been all over the TV and internet. Why are you and Langston Brands thrown into the mix?

Crystal interrupted Layla's firing of questions. "Listen, Lay, I don't have a lot of time. I've been arrested for Dante's murder."

"So did you—"

"Of course, I didn't do it. It's just a misunderstanding that I hope can be squared away in the morning. Marcel is helping me."

"What do you need me to do?"

"Run interference for me—the company, Mom and Dad."

"Crys, all that stuff is secondary. We gotta get you out of there."

"Please, Lay. Try to smooth it over with the board, Mom, and Dad. If they haven't heard about it yet, they will by morning, I'm sure. I'm innocent. I just need our parents to know that."

"Mom and Dad know you're not capable of doing something like this. Don't worry about them. They'll be more concerned about you."

"I can handle this. Marcel will help. I'll give him your number in the morning, too, so be on the lookout for his call."

An automated voice interrupted, alerting her that she had one minute left.

"I gotta go, Lay. Just say a few prayers for me."

Nope.

She would not cry.

Crystal replaced the receiver and followed the officer back to her cell.

If she'd known her night would end up like this, she would've stayed home today. All she'd proven in the eyes of the law was that she was a criminal.

∞

Marcel waited around in the interrogation room for Detective Diggins to return with the results of the gun shot residue test. Crystal didn't fire a gun at Dante, and the results would prove it. He'd get the charges against her dismissed. Afterward, she'd be released from this nightmare.

He flipped his wrist to check the time. The officer took Crystal to be booked two-and-a-half hours ago. Marcel tapped his feet, becoming more impatient and agitated by the second. To keep a calm head and maintain professionalism, he took deep breaths. He had personal reasons to protect Crystal. Tonight was supposed to be his opportunity to express how he's felt about her all these years.

Detective Diggins trekked in the room, interrupting his thoughts, and plopped a folder down on the table.

"Your client is as guilty as they come." Detective Diggins pointed at the folder. "Traces of GSR were found on her wrists."

Marcel picked up the folder. He held his breath while he read the results of the gunshot residue test. His stomach weaved in ways he didn't know it could. Though the test came back positive, the trace count was low.

"Detective, you and I both know that she could've fired a gun at any time today to have this small amount of GSR on her skin. You've got to come with more than that."

"That small amount of GSR, as you put it, coupled with the fact that witnesses have her on video threatening the deceased and entering a room alone with him are enough to charge her. The DA agrees."

"And what did forensics say about her gun? Was it recently fired? Do the bullets match the ones used to kill Mr. Green?"

"We're still waiting, but if I were you, I'd encourage my client to plead guilty and save the government some money."

"My client is innocent. Just be ready to release her as soon as the forensic results come back. See you in the morning, Detective."

Morning couldn't come fast enough for Marcel. Though he and Crystal hadn't been in much contact since college, he was confident enough in her character to know that she wouldn't kill Dante—even if she were carrying around a gun. The most she'd do was attempt to scare him, and if she were to shoot, she wouldn't shoot to kill.

Would she?

That's not the Crystal he knew.

The sooner those results came back, the sooner he and Crystal could move on with their lives. The fact that the sitting DA didn't hesitate to make a decision without all the facts bothered him, but he couldn't place the blame on him. Marcel was certain Detective Diggins played up the evidence he had to push the DA's decision to charge Crystal. This situation was a prime example of why he wanted to secure the DA seat back in Houston—to put real criminals where they belonged.

Crystal was not a criminal.

Seven

Crystal bolted into an upright position at the clanging noise. She blinked to clear her vision. Her back ached, and her body was stiff from that uncomfortable excuse for a mattress. It wasn't a bad dream. She was really in jail.

"You have a visitor."

The officer gestured with his hand, and the door unlocked. He cuffed Crystal and led her to the visitors' area.

A heavy sigh escaped her lips at the sight of Marcel. Hopefully, he came bearing good news. She hid her weary soul behind a smile—one she didn't feel herself.

"Tell me you're getting me out of here. I don't belong in this place, Marcel."

"I'm working on it, Crys, but they found gunshot residue on your wrists. What is that about?"

Crystal puffed up her chest. "I didn't fire that gun last night."

"Calm down. I believe you, but the evidence says you fired a gun at some point yesterday."

Crystal slapped her forehead. "Ah, I did. Yesterday morning, I went to the gun range. In fact, I go to the gun range every Friday morning, usually before work. You can verify that with Jeremy Bennett at The Long Range in Houston."

Marcel jotted down the information.

"Okay. That makes sense."

She sensed relief wash over Marcel when she gave that tidbit of info.

"So what now?"

"They're waiting on forensics to come back with the results of the type of bullet that was used to kill Dante and whether or not that bullet came from your gun."

"It doesn't matter what kind of bullets were used. My clip is full. They'd know that if they checked."

"I know this is hard to hear, but hang on a little longer. We're going to get you out of here."

"I know you will. I need a favor."

"What's that?"

"Call my sister Layla and give her an update to give to my family, and remind her to stay out of this. I don't want my family's name involved any more than it already is." Crystal called out Layla's number for Marcel to key into his contacts.

"Will do. What about Ava?"

"Ava's out of the country securing new buyers for Langston Brands. Let's not bother her with this."

A disapproving look flashed across Marcel's features, but he didn't contest her decision not to include Ava. Crystal knew Ava would be upset once she found out, but she didn't care. It was best to keep her family out of this nonsense as much as possible.

"Is there anything else I should know?"

Crystal shook her head. She pressed her lips together to fight back tears.

Marcel covered her hands with his.

"I will get you out of here. You have my word."

Her voice strained as she said, "As soon as you can."

She battled between helplessness and hope.

Crystal wasn't well versed in law, but understood that if her gun practice yesterday morning wasn't enough to clear her name, hopefully the fact that her clip was full would.

If not, she didn't see any other way out.

∞

Marcel's chest constricted as he stood and watched the jailer escort Crystal out of the visiting room. His heart shattered at the thought of her having to spend another night in this place. Though he'd been in many jail visiting rooms to discuss his clients' cases, the mere thought of being inside the building made his stomach turn and his head throb. He could only imagine what this environment was doing to someone like Crystal who'd never had any reason to come close to a jail. He'd given his word though. He'd do whatever it took to help Crystal. Representing his clients well was what he was good at, and Crystal was by far the most important client he'd ever represented because no one held a piece of his heart like she did.

On his way to the exit, he stopped short after almost colliding with a stunning replica of Crystal, except this woman was about five inches taller with jet-black, long, straight hair.

Marcel cocked his head and raised an eyebrow. Layla Langston. The youngest of the three Langston sisters.

Her words rushed from her lips. "Crystal called me last night. I had to come check on her."

Marcel shook his head, his mind still registering how much Layla resembled her sister. "I was about to call you. Crystal asked me to contact you."

"Well, now I'm here so you don't have to call. How the heck did this happen?" Layla now stood with her fists jammed into her hips. Less than a minute with her, and he could sense the younger sister was bossy. Much like when they were growing up. Crystal's strength lay in her silence, but Layla was sure to let the world know her opinion. Ava fell somewhere in between.

Marcel took hold of her elbow and guided her into a corner.

"It's best that we not speak out in the open like this. I was headed back to my hotel room. You okay with coming to talk?"

Layla nodded, but wore a frown. "That's fine and all, but I have to go see my sister first."

"Okay. I'm working on getting Crystal out of there as soon as possible. But right now, my hands are tied. Crystal had gunshot residue on her wrists, though small, but considering the circumstances, it makes her look guilty. She says she goes to the gun range every Friday, and she went yesterday morning."

Layla threaded her arms across her chest. "That's true. All because of what Dante did to her."

"Right. I need to get a sworn statement or even camera footage, if they have it, to prove that Crystal was there yesterday morning."

Layla whipped out her phone. A shimmer of hope glistened in her eyes. "Done. I can call Uncle Jeremy right now."

"Perfect." Marcel pulled out his phone and sent her a pin to his hotel's location. "I'm in Room 506. Let me know when you're on your way."

Unbelievable how much she and Crystal resembled each other and weren't identical twins. A sinking feeling settled in the pit of his stomach. Even though it had been less than twenty-four hours, it was too long for an innocent person to be in jail. This couldn't go on past today.

Marcel checked out and retraced his steps toward the exit. Though representing criminal cases was what he did for a living, this was no ordinary case, and he couldn't be sure how it would affect his campaign, if at all.

He halted his steps when he made it to the double doors. Reporters and flashing cameras were on the other side. He could see them through the frosted window panels. It didn't take long for the media to find out the police arrested Crystal for Dante's murder. In fact, he'd already received two phone calls this morning requesting a statement.

A heavy breath escaped his lips when he opened the door.

"Mr. Singleton, are you representing Crystal Langston in the murder of the late NFL player, Dante Green?" called one reporter.

"What does the board of Langston Brands have to say about its new CEO being in jail for murder?" shouted another reporter.

"Is it fair to say Ms. Langston plotted to kill Mr. Green as payback for his physical abuse during their marriage?" another reporter asked.

Marcel thrust his palm in the air to quiet the reporters.

"I am representing Ms. Langston, however, at this time, I won't be answering any questions about the ongoing investigation. Thank you."

Marcel maneuvered through the throng of thirsty reporters and cameramen to get back to his car. The second he climbed inside, he pulled off and headed back to his hotel room. His mind turned as fast as the car's wheels on the pavement. Like Crystal, he rented a room last night, but extended his stay after last night's fiasco. He couldn't settle into the comforts of his house until he could get Crystal safely back into her own home.

Marcel navigated back to the hotel, hopped out, and handed the keys to a valet. He looked over his shoulder before he continued his stride through the revolving doors. His mind focused on getting to his room and thumbing through the room service menu. The last thing he should have done was skip breakfast this morning, but thoughts of Crystal in that orange jumpsuit haunted his dreams. With what little sleep he did get, he showered, dressed, and went to see her first thing that morning.

Back inside his room, Marcel took out his phone to call Detective Diggins, but the name glaring on the screen gave him pause. It wasn't unusual for Olivia to call him, but after everything that had happened over the last twenty-four hours, the knot forming in his belly told him he should be worried about what was coming next.

Eight

The jailor escorted Crystal to the visiting area where she had to talk with her visitors through that dirty phone and filthy Plexiglas. No way that was sanitary. Her skin crawled when she walked into the room. The scent of heavy must and pepper spray hung in the air, stinging her nostrils.

Crystal perched on the edge of the chair and lifted the phone with her thumb and forefinger, like that would keep the germs away. She held the phone close enough to her ear without resting it against the side of her face.

She glared into identical eyes and hissed, "Layla, what are you doing here? This isn't part of the plan."

"I think you know me well enough by now to know that I wouldn't stay home while you're sitting inside of a jail cell. I came to make sure you get out of here."

Crystal rolled her eyes. A huge part of her was relieved to see Layla, but she meant what she'd told her earlier. Layla needed to be home to make sure none of this backfired on Langston Brands or her position as the new CEO. Besides, no one needed to see her like this—locked up behind bars for murder. A crime she didn't commit. If anything, her shame wanted to protect Layla. She was the big sister , and though innocent, what kind of example was she setting for Layla and Ava?

"And just how are you planning to do that? I'm sure Marcel is doing everything he can to get me out of here."

"Well, it ain't like he can't use all the help he can get. I'm on your side, Crys, so you know I'm going to do whatever it takes. I'm getting Marcel the timestamped video footage of you entering and leaving the gun range from Uncle Jeremy. That should help speed things up and get you out of here."

Crystal released a steady breath and relaxed in the seat.

"Thanks. How are Mom and Dad taking this horrible news, and please tell me you didn't call Ava?"

Crystal braced herself. Of course her parents knew she wouldn't do anything like this, but knowing she was being held accountable for it couldn't help matters.

Layla pursed her lips like she was looking for a way to break the news to her gently. This couldn't be good.

"Lay?"

"I haven't called Ava yet, but I can't make any promises there. Mom and Dad are okay. They know you're innocent and *ummm,* they trust that I can handle it."

"Handle what? You're not a lawyer."

"True, but I'm checking on things, so to speak, and making sure Marcel does his job."

"Lay, he doesn't need a babysitter. What are you not telling me?"

"Marcel has less than forty-eight hours to get you out of here, or Dad is pulling his support from Marcel's district attorney campaign. And Mom, well, she's trying to smooth things over with the board. We have to delay the unveiling of the new bag collection, and the board isn't pleased. But I don't think you should be concerned about any of that right now."

How could she not be? Langston Brands was her livelihood and the place she found for herself when she left Dante.

"Honestly, my position at Langston Brands is at the forefront of my mind. I've worked hard to get to where I am, and I'm not going to let something like this strip it away from me."

"I know, sis, but remember that we're your family. We've got you. Just stay safe in here."

Crystal looked from her left to her right, her nose slightly turned upward, then faced her sister again. A shiver coursed through her, and she shimmied her shoulders at its release.

"I'm trying. And hey, even though I didn't want you here, I'm glad you came. Marcel might be glad to see you, too."

"We all know he'd move mountains for you if he could, and he doesn't need me around putting pressure on him, but that's exactly what I'm going to do. I don't want you in here anymore than you want to be. Love you, sis."

Like Crystal, Layla didn't want to come into contact with the glass either, and judging from the way she held the phone, she probably got the creeps, too. Layla held her hand up a couple of inches away from the glass. "I'll be in touch."

Crystal held her palm up as well. "Thanks."

Layla stood and replaced the phone. Crystal mirrored her movement.

The jailor opened the door and led Crystal back to her assigned cell. When the iron bars slammed shut, Crystal turned on her heels and knelt against the bed, and for the first time since being imprisoned, she cried.

Ugly cried.

Snotty nose.

Sore throat.

Heaving chest.

She was innocent. But what if for some odd reason, the evidence didn't align with her story? She couldn't serve a prison sentence because she wasn't built for this kind of life. Crystal's body shook. Her belly ached. She sobbed until her head ached. When she could pull herself together, she did what she hadn't done in a while: prayed.

Lord God, I don't even know what to say. I'm not sure how my life ended up in such a mess. Forgive my pride and my desire to do things my way. Please give Marcel wisdom to do his part in helping me get out of this place. I ask for your protection and your grace. In Jesus' name, Amen.

∞

"Liv." Marcel answered the video call and braced himself for whatever news she had. Air trapped in his chest, his stomach taut.

"Murder?" she blurted without saying hello first.

Based on her reaction, he'd think the murder charges were against him, not Crystal.

"She didn't do it, and I'm going to make sure she gets out of jail. Crys won't be paying for a crime she didn't commit if I have anything to say about it."

"*Hmmm.*" Olivia paced and wagged a finger in the air. "Good thinking taking on her case. This is good for your campaign."

Marcel released his pent-up breath. He didn't choose to help Crystal to boost his chances of winning the race for district attorney.

"Really? How can you be sure?" He sat at the desk inside his hotel room, crossed an ankle over his knee, and nodded for Olivia to continue.

"Trust me. I've been doing this for a long time. A pro football player is dead. Everyone will be watching the outcome of this murder case and how you handle it, and if they didn't know who you were before, they'll know now and get a glimpse into what you're all about. This is your chance to prove what you stood in front of that audience and said yesterday. You're serious about putting the right people behind bars, not the innocent."

Marcel massaged his chin with his thumb and forefinger, his thoughts running rampant. "I trust you, Liv."

"Good. Just know this has the potential to make or break your campaign."

"I got this, and if that's the situation, I have a feeling this is going to be good for both of us. I'm pretty sure you'll be more sought after since you're my campaign manager."

Olivia chuckled and jabbed a finger at the screen. "You just concentrate on taking care of Crystal while making yourself look good. This is bigger than her. It's about you, too."

That's where he was conflicted.

He didn't want to make this case about him. This should be an open-and-shut case. Ensure the ballistic report came back clean. Get Crystal released. Focus on the district attorney race and seeing if there was a future for him and Crystal together.

"Got it. Let me get to work, then. I'll touch base with you on Monday as planned."

"Talk to you soon."

Marcel ended the call. He'd missed Layla's message telling him she was on her way. His stomach growled at the sound of three taps on the door. He advanced to the door in four steps. His shoulders dropped when he saw Layla and not room service. After stepping aside to allow her into the room, he peeked around the corner for any sign of the room service staff. Where was his food?

"That was fast."

"I just needed to put eyes on my sister to make sure she was doing okay. I talked to Uncle Jeremy on the way over. He's e-mailing the video footage of Crystal entering and leaving the range on Friday morning. That should be enough, right?"

The hope in her eyes matched that of Crystal's when she talked about them checking her gun to corroborate her story. She had a full round.

"It should be enough, especially when the ballistic report comes back."

"Good. I'll forward it to you as soon as he sends it to me." She shoved her phone into his palm. "Type in your e-mail so we can make sure you get it."

Marcel's stomach growled as he typed.

"Detective Diggins wasn't in the office when I went to visit Crystal this morning. I'm going to pay him a visit after I grab a bite to eat. I'll touch base with you then."

Layla spun on her heels and retreated toward the door.

Marcel called out to her. “Hey. I’m a little surprised to see you as opposed to your father. What’s the deal with him?”

Layla shrugged. “Oh, he’s not happy at all. Said he’d pull his financial support from your campaign if you didn’t get Crystal out of jail by Monday morning.”

She left him standing in the middle of the room, not giving him a chance to respond.

Nine

Marcel committed to getting results—or at least answers—today. He made himself comfortable at the precinct, waiting for Detective Diggins to return to his office. He was out investigating another crime, but Marcel didn't care. He brought a cup of coffee and his iPad, which had kept him occupied for the last hour and a half. News reporters lurked outside, but thankfully, they didn't bum rush him with questions about whether Crystal would be formally charged for Dante's murder. When he was ready to give a statement, he wanted to be able to say his client was innocent as evidenced by her release.

"Attorney Singleton, sorry to have kept you waiting." The detective's vocal presence entered the room before he did.

Marcel doubted Detective Diggins' sincerity, but nodded and said, "No problem. This is the only thing on my agenda today."

Detective Diggins gripped Marcel's hand in a firm shake before rounding his desk to sit. He slid his fingers across the keyboard to log into his computer.

"I sent over the video footage that shows Ms. Langston entering and leaving The Lone Range yesterday morning, which proves why she had GSR particles on her wrist last night."

Marcel watched Detective Diggins review the footage, exit the video, and then click another message. He remained quiet while he checked his inbox. Marcel took his silence to mean that whatever e-mail he was reading had something to do with his client.

After the extended stretch of silence, Marcel asked, "Detective, do you have the forensic ballistic results yet?"

Detective Diggins took several seconds to respond, too long in Marcel's opinion. He completed his task of clicking through a message, made a show of leaning back against his seat, and adjusted his suspenders.

"Ms. Langston is free to go."

Every muscle in Marcel's body softened, however, he needed more information. "I appreciate that, Detective, but I need more. Tell me the results of the ballistic report."

Detective Diggins clasped his hands together and shifted his weight on the desk. He narrowed his eyes, which made Marcel believe he wouldn't like what he'd say next.

"While the bullet that killed the victim matches the same type of bullets in Ms. Langston's gun, the report says her gun wasn't fired last night. In full transparency, though the evidence corroborates her story, I still don't believe she's innocent. Maybe she conspired with someone else."

He squinted at Marcel like the pieces to the puzzle could be solved from something in his face. Detective Diggins slapped both hands on the desk. "But I can't prove that just yet. She's free to go, but definitely not off my list."

"Don't spend the government's money looking in the wrong direction, Detective."

Marcel gathered his things, left Detective Diggins' office, and walked to the front of the building to wait for Crystal. He whipped out to his phone to call Layla to share the good news and that he would take her home.

This nightmare was over.

∞

Freedom felt good.

It was one of those things she undervalued until she lost it.

Crystal didn't think she'd ever changed clothes as fast as she did. In thirty seconds, she was out of that orange jumpsuit and back into the dress she wore last night. Maybe less. After everything she'd gone through, she'd burn the dress. It held too many sour memories—memories she wanted to forget after today.

Her encounter with Dante.

His death.

Her time in jail.

She just wanted—well, needed—to forget the last few days.

She signed the paperwork for her belongings confiscated from her at booking, accepted her purse, jewelry, and gun, and raced toward the exit where she spotted Marcel standing near the front door.

She held his neck in a death grip. "Thank you."

"You're welcome. I wouldn't have it any other way." She could feel his warm breath in her hair.

Not wanting to spend another millisecond in the building, she released him and tugged him through the exit, where reporters and cameras awaited.

She rubbed her arms to stave off the chill because she was clothed in the same dress she wore to the reunion's mixer. The cooler temperature didn't bother her. Nor did the media.

She was free.

Marcel stopped before descending the steps. So many different questions were coming from every direction. It was maddening, but Marcel's steady hand on her back comforted her.

He raised his hand, and the reporters quieted. Microphones jutted in their direction.

"Ms. Langston did not murder Mr. Dante Green. I'm pleased to announce that law enforcement has released my client after the evidence has corroborated her innocence. No further comments. Thank you."

Marcel led her to his car, opened the door for her, and rounded the bumper to climb behind the wheel once she was safely inside.

"Where to?"

"The Hilton."

Crystal released a loud sigh when Marcel drove off and settled into the leather seat. Far more comfortable than the confines of the police cruiser she rode in a couple of nights ago. She silently prayed she'd never have to experience that again.

"I'm sorry I couldn't get you out faster, but we had to wait on the ballistic results to prove the bullets didn't come from your gun. It also helped that we had video of you going to The Lone Range yesterday to support why you would have gunshot residue on your wrist."

"I'm just glad everything worked out. I don't think I've ever been so happy to see you."

Marcel chuckled a bit before saying, "I'm not sure if I should be offended or not."

They exchanged a glance. The tenderness Crystal saw in his eyes evoked feelings she shouldn't have for her friend. "Trust me. It's a compliment."

Crystal patted Marcel's arm. "I'm so thankful for you, you know that, right? I'm not sure how this would've turned out without you here."

"You do know that if I weren't here, all you had to do was call, and I would have found a way to help you."

Crystal nodded. Even after all this time with little communication with Marcel, she knew what he said to be true. It was something about the way he said it and the way his eyes bore into hers when he said it. Her body felt it, too, because a shiver shot through her core.

The twenty-minute drive back to the hotel seemed to take forever. Though Marcel was good company, she was ready to get home. Her home. Her bed. Her garden bathtub. Safety. All were calling to her.

When they arrived at the hotel, Crystal arranged to meet Marcel in twenty minutes. Inside her room, she gave herself a once-over in the mirror. She at least needed to shower and change clothes.

Water streams from the showerhead were like a taste of heaven, but she couldn't linger. After a few minutes, she was out of there, toweled off, and dressed in a matching yoga outfit. She threw her clothes in her suitcase, not caring if they were packed neatly as she normally would have. All that mattered was that it closed.

She gathered her purse, keys, and cell phone. Now all she had to do was check out. On her way to the door, she noticed a white sheet of paper on the floor. One less thing to do, the hotel had already checked her out.

Crystal picked the hotel receipt up off the floor and was about to stuff it into her purse, until she realized the hotel logo wasn't there. Only a few words were in large, bold print: **You'll wish you stayed in jail by the time I'm done with you.**

Ten

Thirty minutes into their drive, and Crystal barely spoke. Marcel had even tried some of his best jokes, but they weren't enough. She'd laugh, but then retreat. Marcel assumed that the jail ordeal, work, and what awaited her at Langston Brands monopolized her thoughts, but it had to be more than that. He caught her fidgeting from time to time. And at one point, he was certain she wiped a tear from her eye. Were those tears for Dante?

Yet, she hadn't opened up to him.

Since they left the hotel, she seemed shaky, or scared even. But again, he assumed it had to do with everything that transpired over the weekend.

They stopped to refill the gas tank. When Marcel climbed back into the car after refueling, he shifted in his seat to face her.

"Crys, I know something's bothering you, and I don't mind being a listening ear."

Crystal rubbed her hands along her pant leg. She glanced up at him, but didn't speak. She fidgeted with her fingers again.

"Okay. I know my jokes aren't that bad. Would you rather listen to music?"

He didn't mind the silence, but it wasn't that natural silence between friends who were comfortable with each other. This quietness seemed thick and heavy, like something was bothering her.

Crystal cleared her throat. "I don't know what to say. I suppose I could just show you." She opened her purse, pulled out a white sheet of paper, and handed it to him.

Air constricted in his chest.

His voice raised an octave. "Where'd you get this?"

"It was under the door in my hotel room when I got out of the shower."

Marcel wanted to be upset with her. Why didn't she show this to him before they left? He knew the answer to that: Crystal wanted this all behind her. And there wasn't much they could do about it anyway. Maybe ask the hotel for their camera footage to see who slid the note under the door. Perhaps take it down to Detective Diggins and have him run fingerprints.

Marcel kept his voice even. "What do you think this means? Do you have any idea who could have left this note for you?"

"I think someone wanted me to take the fall for Dante's murder. Now that I've been released from jail, it's more likely the cops will find the real killer who could be the person who sent this note."

"I'm calling Detective Diggins."

Crystal reached over and grabbed his wrist, her strength surprising him, but not more surprising than that prickling in his chest every time she touched him. "No, don't. Let's just go home and put all the drama of the last couple of days behind us."

"Since when did you stop taking your attorney's advice?"

"I'm pretty sure you're off payroll now that I'm out of jail."

Marcel studied her for several seconds, nearly getting lost in the depths of her eyes. He shook his head to fight the feelings that threatened to resurface. Dante must have known way back then that he had feelings for Crystal. Why hadn't she ever noticed? But this was neither the time nor place to even think about such things. Her ex-husband was now dead, which added trauma to what was already there due to Crystal and Dante's troubled relationship. Surely, she wouldn't be ready for anything with him now.

He couldn't be so sure he was ready either.

"Diggins still has his eyes on you, though, and I'm going to do whatever it takes for him to shift his focus. I need to call him."

"Wait. Why is he still looking at me? I've been cleared. I'm not a suspect anymore."

"Formally, you're not, but that doesn't mean you're in the clear if he suspects you're guilty. His theory is that you were probably working with someone. Some type of vindictive jealous ex-wife motive is my guess."

Crystal shook her head, confusion evident in the way her eyes grew larger. "But what would I have to gain from Dante's death?"

"I'm sure that's what he's trying to figure out. I know you're innocent, so it's important that we stay in front of this."

She leaned back against her seat. Her face relaxed. Crystal waved her hand. "Make the call."

Marcel retrieved his phone out of the center console, tapped, and swiped until the detective's name appeared on his screen. He touched the call icon and switched on the speaker so Crystal could listen to the conversation.

When the detective answered, Marcel took a deep breath. Why hadn't Crystal said anything about this when she first discovered the note? Marcel was certain that would be the detective's line of thinking.

"Detective, Attorney Singleton here. I have a bit of information for you." Marcel retold the story as Crystal shared it with him and waited for Detective Diggins' response.

"I'll look into it."

The detective's earlier conviction about Crystal's innocence hovered in Marcel's thoughts like a helicopter waiting to land. How serious would he take this information? Marcel had the mind to investigate the note himself, but that wasn't his job. He had to trust Detective Diggins to use his resources to determine what was happening.

Besides, he had a campaign that needed his attention.

"Thanks. Please call me when you find any information. My client's personal safety could be at risk."

"I'll be in touch."

∞

Lord, please make all of this go away.

Crystal watched Marcel finish his call with Detective Diggins. From the beginning, she sensed the detective had it in for her, but she was innocent, and the evidence proved it. She prayed this note situation would lead the cops to the real killer and get them off her scent so she could ease back into her normal life.

She reached out for Marcel's hand and squeezed.

"I know this isn't what you had in mind for your twentieth college reunion weekend, but I appreciate you being there for me. I've said it before, but it's worth saying again: Let me know if there's anything I can do to repay you, other than your fee—and no discounts."

Marcel chuckled. When he sobered, his expression softened, and he looked at her in a way he'd never done before. Crystal's heart skipped a beat. Several.

"How about dinner?"

Crystal's breath caught.

"Whenever you're ready. No rush."

She was seconds away from melting in that leather seat, thanks to Marcel's I'd-do-anything-for-you smile. He didn't say it, but she felt it.

Physically.

Her heart revved with the turning of the engine.

"I think I'd like that."

"It's the one thing I think we owe ourselves." Marcel navigated the car back onto the freeway before he continued. "But I do understand you've been through a lot. There's no reason for you to rush into anything with me—or anyone else."

He'd glimpsed at her when he tagged on *anyone else.*

"Whatever you're thinking, stop thinking it. Relationships have not even been on my radar since Dante and I ended our marriage, and I'm not the kind of woman who thinks all men are like him or would hurt me the way he did. I want to make sure I make the right choice next go-round, if at all."

Marcel nodded, his head movement slow and rhythmic. Crystal took the opportunity to share what she hadn't with anyone else, not even her sisters though they probably had some idea anyway.

"You know, Marcel, I've always considered myself to be strong and smart—an independent and capable woman. That's who my parents raised me to be, and I still can't get over how I fell for someone like him. How did I miss—or why did I ignore—all the signs?"

"Like many other women, you probably thought your goodness could change him."

"Ha. That was rhetorical."

"Maybe, but I'd like to think you mentioned it so you could get my opinion."

He took his eyes off the road for a moment and bore into hers in a way that made her want to turn into a puddle, and all it took was two seconds.

When and how did this attraction come about with her friend?

Perhaps because he'd just helped her through a traumatic experience. But that couldn't be true. Her emotions betrayed her the moment he stood before his crowd of donors and gave his campaign speech.

Crystal shifted in her seat and took in his profile. Skin smooth and dark like milk chocolate, her favorite dessert. Strong jawline. And full lips that she wouldn't mind… She fluttered her eyelids and shook the thoughts out of her head.

What was wrong with her?

"Well, sounds like you've got it all figured out. What else you got?"

He squinted and twisted his lips. She could tell he was trying to determine whether he should say what came to mind.

"Oh, don't hold back on me now."

Marcel released a half-hearted chuckle. "I just never understood what you saw in him."

She parted her lips to defend herself, but Marcel wasn't finished.

"Especially when you had me in your life."

"Wow."

Those tiny bumps popped up along her arms, reminding her of the conversation they'd had at the reunion when he mentioned having to wait so long to dance with her. So many thoughts muddled her mind. Just how much was Marcel into her when they were growing up? When did this attraction start? And should anything be done about it now? Or ever?

Crystal fingered her collarbone and thought for a moment.

Tread carefully.

"Are you serious?"

"I wouldn't kid about that. I get it. You friend-zoned me early on—way back in elementary school."

Crystal laughed at the memory.

"We were like nine. I'm pretty sure neither one of us knew anything about relationships back then."

"I'm glad you find it funny."

Marcel joined her in laughter.

"But for real. By the time we were seniors in high school, I got the picture. You laughed at the idea of us going to prom together."

Crystal pressed her palm to her chest. Her eyes grew wider at the memory. She sucked in a loud breath. "You were serious? I didn't think you were, and that could have been the way you presented it to me. Always joking around. Shoot, as far as I was concerned, I thought you were taking pity on me since I didn't have a date and planned to go with a group of girlfriends."

Marcel turned his lips downward in what she assumed was a playful pout and shook his head. "You think so little of me."

Crystal squeezed his arm. "You're one of the few people I think highly of."

Marcel looked at her and shifted one eyebrow upward.

She should really stop touching him. They hadn't been physically or emotionally close in years before this weekend, yet it seemed as if no time had passed. Her feelings were increasingly jumbling by the second.

Was she sending the wrong message?

Probably.

She didn't even know what message she wanted to send.

∞

Every time he felt Crystal's touch, it reminded him of the lost opportunity between them.

Reminded him of buried feelings.

And reminded him that he hadn't done a good job of suppressing them.

With every moment in the car with just the two of them, he couldn't help but think about old times. Or how he didn't want to lose her again.

But she'd just gone through a traumatic ordeal. And though she and Dante's relationship had been over for more than a year, she still had to experience some grief, yet she showed no signs. Was she in denial?

Further, was he pushing too hard, too fast? In his defense, he did say that they could go to dinner when she was ready. He hadn't planned to ask her out. At least not yet. The moment overtook him, and he didn't want to lose the opportunity again. If they parted ways this evening and he didn't see her for another long period of time, he hoped she knew that he once and still did have feelings for her.

"I can go on now knowing that you think highly of me."

Crystal laughed. He loved seeing her like that. Carefree. Joyful. But he couldn't help but think she was holding back her feelings. Whatever the case, he hoped to be around when she needed that shoulder to cry on.

She sobered and retrieved her buzzing phone from her purse. Her hands trembled. The next thing he saw was her phone tumbling to the floor. Marcel glanced over and caught her panic-stricken face. Her mouth hung open. She turned to look at him with those wide eyes.

"What's the matter?"

Her voice cracked. "Another threatening message."

Eleven

Who was this person, and what did they want? What fulfillment did they get out of taunting her?

Crystal attempted using breathing techniques to calm her nerves. When that didn't work, she slipped both hands beneath her legs to hide the trembles.

She kept her gaze fixated on the road ahead. "Someone is playing a silly mind game with me, that's all."

Did she successfully hide the fear in her voice? To her own ears, she could barely hear the trembling. Had Marcel bought it?

"What did the text say?"

"Going home won't stop what's coming to you. Marcel can't save you either."

Marcel nodded, his head moving in a slow, thoughtful manner. She could tell he was working up a way to figure this whole thing out.

"Whoever this is knew where you were staying, which also means it was likely someone at the reunion."

"Why would anyone want to kill Dante and frame me for it?"

"That's what the cops need to find out. We need to get the number and get it to Detective Diggins to have him trace it. If this person is smart, it's probably a burner. It doesn't hurt to try though."

Crystal stared down at the phone on the car floor like it was covered in bugs. How did these people even get her number? How far would he or she take their threats? Was this someone who lived in Houston? She spent several seconds thinking through the classmates she knew who lived in the area, but she didn't keep in touch with many, except a few sorority sisters. Then there was Marcel and Jacob, Dante's agent. She immediately discounted the fact he could be involved. They'd mostly had a cordial relationship with him even calling to check on her after she and Dante divorced. Crystal leaned over, and picked up her phone.

If she had to guess, this person was a woman. It just seemed unlikely that a man would be sending those kinds of messages to her.

Marcel used his fingerprint to unlock his phone and handed it to Crystal.

"Call Detective Diggins and put the phone on speaker. I'll talk to him and tell him about what has happened."

Crystal opened Marcel's call log and tapped on Detective Diggins' number. She listened while Marcel recounted the details of the message Crystal had received. His voice was firm, calm, and in control, the opposite of how she felt right now—shaky, confused, and terrified.

When he finished, Detective Diggins said, "Give me the number and send me a screenshot of the message."

Crystal opened her messages and recited the number to him. Afterwards she sent the screenshot to the number Detective Diggins called out to her.

"Thanks. I'll see what we can dig up. And just so you know, my partner is on his way to the hotel to view camera footage. Notify me immediately if anything else comes up, no matter how insignificant you think it may be."

Marcel nodded, not that Detective Diggins could see him. "Will do. Thanks."

Detective Diggins thanked the two of them once more and ended the call.

She must not have been doing a decent job of hiding her feelings because Marcel reached over and secured her hand in his.

"Everything is going to be fine. I won't let anyone hurt you, Crys."

As comforting as his sentiments were, he couldn't be there for her twenty-four-seven. He wasn't her bodyguard. He had a life that had been devoid of her until a few days ago. And Marcel had his campaign to give his time and energy to, so there was no time for him to not let anyone hurt her.

But Crystal was a grown and capable woman. She could handle herself. Hadn't she been preparing to protect herself over the last year through countless hours at the gun range? And self-defense classes? So why did it feel like her stomach was weighed down by an anchor right now?

Crystal saved the screenshot for evidence and blocked the number.

"Thank you. I won't let anything happen to me either." *Never again.*

"It's okay to let me be here for you. You know that, right? We know you're a strong woman, but we don't know who or what we're dealing with. What if these threats are real?"

That's what she was afraid of.

∞

Letting go of Crystal's hand was the last thing he wanted to do. For the past fifteen minutes, her hand rested in his. She hadn't moved, and neither did he. Did it feel as natural to her as it did to him? It was like they were meant to hold hands. For the life of him, he wasn't sure why touching Crystal was affecting him like this. He touched her hands a thousand times over the years, but now every suppressed feeling threatened to manifest itself. Before he did or said something crazy, Marcel released her hand and gripped the steering wheel.

The ringtone assigned to his sister and campaign manager, Olivia, cut through the comfortable silence. Thank goodness, because his thoughts were set to start a rollercoaster ride. He answered and put the phone on speaker.

"Hey, Liv. I'm in the car with Crystal, and you're on speaker, so don't embarrass me."

"Hey, Crystal."

"Hey, Olivia."

Marcel caught the smile gracing Crystal's features, and a solid thud slammed in his chest. He shook his head. *Get it together.*

"When have I ever embarrassed you? I've always made you look good."

"I guess you have a point." Marcel chuckled. That was why he'd hired her to be his campaign manager. She'd worked wonders for everyone else's campaign she managed. He had no doubt she could help him secure the coveted DA seat. "What's up?"

"Just calling to remind you about the student town hall at Texas Southern Monday night. With everything that's happened over the weekend, are you still up for it? I need to know ASAP if you need to cancel."

"I'll be there. Six-thirty, right?"

"Right. Hey, Crystal, you should come. Are you busy Monday evening?"

Olivia took the words out of his mouth because the moment she mentioned the event, thoughts of Crystal being there to support him surfaced.

Crystal's gaze lingered on him before she answered. "I'm not sure, but I think I can make arrangements to be there."

"I hope you can. It would be great to see you. Maybe we can catch up over a late dinner once we're done at the town hall."

"I think we have a plan. See you Monday."

Though the extra time with her came by way of an invitation from Olivia, more of Crystal was just what the doctor ordered.

"Perfect. Where are you guys now?" Olivia asked.

Marcel glanced at the GPS. "About twenty minutes from Crystal's house."

"Okay. Be safe, and send me a text when you make it home. I'll catch up with you tomorrow morning."

"Sounds good. Later."

Not only did he get to spend more time with Crystal, but her being at the town hall event also meant that he'd have eyes on her. Knew she was safe. Knew that he'd be right there if she needed him.

"Thanks for agreeing to attend the townhall. I know you have enough to deal with right now, so it means a lot to me."

"That's what friends are for. You've had my back this weekend, so I've got yours."

There went that sweet, soul-stirring smile again.

"That's what's up."

Marcel couldn't relish in the moment they were sharing because the sound of a speeding car drew his attention. He glanced in his rearview mirror. He was driving eighty miles per hour, but the car closing in on them had to be doing at least one hundred. With a wide-open passing lane, it seemed strange that the car didn't switch lanes, so Marcel signaled and moved to the passing lane.

The driver followed.

Marcel swerved back into the right lane.

The driver followed and accelerated even more.

"I think we're being followed—or someone is really crazy."

Crystal looked in the side view mirror. "They're coming really fast."

Adrenaline pumped through Marcel's veins. His heart raced. Thoughts of the messages Crystal had received plowed through his thoughts. Was the driver the person behind the note and the text? It seemed crazy to even consider, but why else would this be happening right now?

Marcel accelerated, and the car behind them did the same.

Seconds before collision, the car swerved to the left lane and sped past them, inches from grazing the driver's side door.

Twelve

The threatening messages and almost being run down on the interstate left Crystal paranoid. Marcel drove her home, saw her safely inside, and insisted on checking her home for things that may be out of place, even though she had a house alarm. According to the alarm app, there were no disturbances or heat signatures picked up on the cameras. He didn't want to take any chances though. Once satisfied that she was okay, he left.

Now the deafening silence made her mind race. She couldn't unsee the note under her hotel room door or the text message. Crystal doublechecked the front and back door locks, then set her alarm. She tossed the reunion dress in the trash and the rest of her clothes into the laundry room. After not getting restful sleep for the past few nights, she soaked in her tub before she settled for an early bedtime.

But she couldn't sleep.

After an hour of tossing and turning, she climbed out of bed, brewed a cup of tea, and went to her home office. She turned on the heating pad and nestled into her leather office chair. The warmth on her back combined with the hot cup of tea relaxed her. She sipped her tea, flipped open her laptop, and closed her eyes for a moment. Clearer thoughts danced in her mind.

Crystal signed in to check e-mail. Hopefully by the time she finished her tea, she'd be calm and relaxed enough for sleep. Working and the feeling of accomplishment often did the trick, too. After the terrible weekend she'd had, taking care of anything on behalf of her family's designer handbag company, Langston Brands, would likely make her feel better.

Have they already discussed a new launch date for the new handbag collection?

But as soon as the thought crossed her mind, her belly sank. The few sips of tea she drank sloshed around. The subject line CEO Removal caught her attention first. There was at least a chain of ten e-mails. She swallowed to moisten her drying throat.

Why would they want to remove her?

She was innocent.

The charges were dropped.

This entire ordeal was supposed to be behind her.

She grabbed her cell phone and called Langston Brands' public relations chair, her sister, Layla.

Layla picked up on the first ring.

"What's going on, Lay?" Crystal couldn't bring herself to open the messages.

"You made it home yet?"

"Yeah. Sorry about not calling. Got distracted. And thanks for going through all the trouble of taking an Uber out there to pick up my car and drop it off at my house."

"You're welcome. Just remember my selfless act when I need something from you."

They shared a laugh. Crystal didn't have any doubt Layla would call in her favor.

Forcing herself to bring up the more serious questions, Crystal asked, "But what's going on at the company? Why is there discussion about removing me from my position?"

"I wouldn't worry about that too much. This will all blow over soon."

"But I need to know so we can deal with the now. I don't want to wait until soon comes. If this is about Dante, I'm innocent, so what's the deal?"

Crystal could hear Layla's loud sigh through the line. "Bad press. It doesn't look good for the CEO to be a murder suspect. Dad is dealing with it, though."

"I would find comfort in that if we didn't have shareholders to answer to." And to think, it was Crystal's idea to issue an initial public offering and go public. The ink wasn't even dry on the paperwork. They'd only been a public company three months now.

"True, but have you forgotten that our family is on the board of directors?"

"Yeah, I know, but I'm still not feeling this. How did this come about anyway? Give me names."

"Let's just say that certain members of the board aren't very happy about the direction the company is headed because its CEO was accused of murder. The idea is if Langston Brands can do damage control by replacing you, we can quickly bounce back."

Crystal pressed her forehead in her palms, then massaged her temples.

Though she didn't necessarily want Dante to die, a small part of her was glad he would no longer be a threat to her in any way—happy that she could move on. But how could she do that when his death has now caused at least two problems: the threats on her life and the possibility of losing her job?

Lord, please make this go away.

"I can't believe this is happening to me." Crystal's strained voice was foreign, even to her ears.

"It's gonna get better. We'll get this taken care of so you can have some peace."

"Thanks."

Why was she thanking Layla? Was there really anything Layla could do for her in this situation? Layla didn't hold her fate at their family's company in her hands. Crystal understood the business, though. Image was important in their industry, so as the CEO, she couldn't do anything that would make the company look bad.

"Try to get some rest. I'll see you bright and early in the office Monday morning."

Crystal hesitated. She wasn't quite finished talking, but what more could be said? "Okay. Good night."

She ended the call not feeling any better than she did before she talked to Layla. In fact, she felt worse. The heaviness now weighed on her shoulders and in her belly like a ship's anchor in the middle of the sea.

She reached to close the laptop lid, but an e-mail notification came through from her administrative assistant. The subject line read, *Monday Schedule Cleared to Meet with Board of Directors.*

How could she even sleep with this hanging over her head?

And more importantly, how would she fight back?

∞

"So when did you assign yourself the position of Crystal's bodyguard? Be straight up with me, and tell me what's really going on with you two."

Oliva's tone dropped several octaves to emphasize her point when she said *really going on.*

"*Hmmmph.* Crys has been my friend for a long time. You know that. I would've represented any of my friends who went through the same thing she did over the weekend. No biggie."

"Do me a favor and look at the caller's name on your phone."

"What?"

"Exactly. Do you know who you're talking to? I'm your sister. Your blood. Keep it real. You're still holding that little torch for her, huh?"

Torch wouldn't be the word he'd use. Just an unexplored infatuation, but he wouldn't tell his sister as much. The chemistry between them seemed deeper than that whenever they touched.

"That's not important. I thought you wanted to talk to me about the campaign."

"Okay. I'll let you slide this time, but you better fess up soon unless you want me to open my big mouth and ask her about it at dinner tomorrow night."

Marcel chuckled. "A risk I'm willing to take. Whatcha got for me?"

He busied himself tossing his dirty clothes into his laundry room and shoving his suitcase into the master bedroom closet while Olivia talked about using recent events to support his campaign platform.

"Whether you like it or not, it's going to come up in conversation and questions. You have to remember that people are nosey, but trust me, they will use the Crystal and Dante angle, so you may as well get in front of the ball."

"Liv, I get that, but I just feel like this is too personal. If we decide to go in this direction, I'd like to talk with Crys about it first so that she's prepared."

"Big bro, it's already happening. I've been filtering calls about this case since news broke that you were defending her, and she should be used to being in the spotlight since she was married to an NFL player. She must have done hundreds of interviews, statements, and photoshoots. I think she'll be okay with it."

Marcel chose not to share news of the recent threats with Olivia. Though Crystal might have experience in the spotlight, he knew she wanted the Dante business behind her. On top of that, didn't she need time to grieve?

"I'm not sure about it. Just give me some time to talk to her before we make a move."

Olivia released an exasperated sigh, one Marcel could feel through the phone line. He rolled his eyes heavenward.

"Okay, but remember you signed up for this. You gotta play the game, and if possible, talk to her before you get to tomorrow's town hall, especially since she's planning to be there. I'm warning you now that the questions will probably go sideways with people going on a fishing expedition."

"Don't worry, Liv. I can handle the questions."

"I know you can, but you hired me to help you win this election, so package your feelings for Crystal and put them on the shelf."

"There you go again. Good night. I'll call you tomorrow."

Marcel shook his head and ended the call. Olivia was on a fishing expedition of her own trying to figure out what was going on with him and Crystal. He couldn't answer because he didn't know either.

Thirteen

Thanks to thoughts of her impending removal as CEO of Langston Brands, Crystal didn't sleep much, if at all, the rest of the weekend. She'd already lost so much because of her relationship with Dante, starting with some friends in college. While they were married, she mingled mostly with other NFL players' wives, but never formed a connection, felt welcomed, or like she fit in with that crowd. That left her isolated and lonely most days. When she decided to leave her abusive marriage with Dante, she started over and put her degree to use—something she allowed Dante to talk her out of when they first married. She wound up spending most of her time supporting him and leading fundraising events in his name to make him look good.

She found the courage to walk away, start fresh, rebuild her life, and lead her family's company like she'd planned the moment she enrolled in Houston University. Now look at her, still trying to get away from her past.

Crystal patted makeup on her face, paying special attention to hide the puffiness around her eyes.

Even though she was alone in her home, she whispered to her reflection in the mirror, "Dante, I won't let you take my career from me. I've already given you enough."

Her hand shook while she worked to apply mascara, so much so, that she dropped the brush on the countertop. An eerie feeling washed over her entire being, like Dante's spirit was in the bathroom with her. Crystal's heart thudded in her chest. She sucked in a few heavy breaths. Knowing she was alone, she still stepped away from the sink and checked inside the closet and master bedroom for another presence.

Reminded and comforted by the fact she was still alone after seeing no one, she released several calming breaths.

"Get it together."

Her stomach churned when she considered she might lose her CEO position at Langston Brands in the next couple of hours. Her phone's loud vibration on the marble vanity countertop stole her attention from her wayward thoughts.

Marcel.

She gave the kind of smile she hadn't recognized on herself in a while. Was that the kind of look she'd been giving him when he drove her home?

"Hey. Good morning."

"Morning, Crys. Been thinking about you since I got up. How was your night?"

"Restless." She considered hiding her true feelings but that wouldn't do her any good.

She finished off her makeup and walked into the master bedroom to sit in her reading chair to compose and calm herself. Marcel's voice through the line nearly did the trick, however.

"Sorry about that. Wanna grab lunch today and talk about it?"

"Sounds good. I might be more than free."

"I don't like the way you said that. Sure you don't need to talk now?"

Crystal was one who believed in the power of words, so she resisted the urge to talk about her meeting with the board and what may come of it before it happened. As many times as she talked to Marcel yesterday, she avoided the work conversation. "No, not yet. I'll just see how the morning goes. I'll have plenty to chat about over lunch, I'm sure. How was the rest of your evening?"

"I had a talk with Olivia about my campaign last night, and she has an interesting idea. I'd like to run it by you first, but that's also a conversation that can wait until we meet for lunch. Have a great morning, and give me a call when you're ready to meet. We can meet in Midtown."

"That works for me. I'll call you in a bit."

When Crystal ended the call, she retraced her steps back into the restroom to get her favorite pair of tear drop pearl earrings. She caught a glimpse of herself in the mirror and that same goofy smile was plastered across her face.

Recognition dawned in her eyes. She'd been giving Marcel that same smile at the reunion and in the car ride back to her house.

For goodness' sake, Marcel was her friend. Where was all of this coming from?

∞

Walking the plank.

That's what Crystal felt like walking through the corporate offices of Langston Brands. The tension in the office was so thick that an obsidian blade knife couldn't slice through it. Normally, her employees would greet her with smiles and good mornings. Obviously, they'd heard about what happened to her over the weekend. The security guards' eyes were sympathetic when she walked through the lobby downstairs, but it seemed every person she passed beyond the security point held judgment in their eyes. At least that's the vibe she was getting. No one smiled.

Except her receptionist, Patrice Wilkins.

And even her smile seemed pretentious.

She rounded her L-shaped cherry oak desk outside of Crystal's office and stood at attention, like Crystal had orders for her.

She didn't.

Crystal wasn't too certain of her own fate.

"Good morning, Patrice." On a normal Monday, Patrice would be prepared to bring Crystal her morning cup of coffee and settle into one of the visitor's chairs for their weekly status updates and to review Crystal's calendar for the week.

But Patrice's wide-eyed look told Crystal that today would be different.

Everyone knew today was different.

Their boss had spent part of the weekend behind bars.

"Do you need anything? The board is already waiting in the Hobo conference room."

All the conference rooms were named after different handbag styles—Satchel, Tote, Wristlet, Clutch, and Crossbody—and like the size of the bag, the Tote conference room was the largest and big enough to comfortably sit their two hundred employees. The Satchel held about one hundred. The Crossbody and Hobo could both seat twenty-five people. The Wristlet and Clutch were the two smallest rooms, which could seat about ten people. Though the board could have chosen one of those rooms today, Crystal was glad they didn't.

The air around her already seemed stuffy. No need to be in such a tight space contributing to her anxiety, although the nine board members could comfortably occupy the room.

The Hobo room was her favorite, if she had to choose. With two oversized conference room tables, it was casual and inviting, a lot less intimidating than the others. Snacks and coffee were often already in place. Two flat-screen TVs hung on both ends of the room. Six vases of fresh flowers adorned the middle and each end of both tables. On top of that, the view of downtown Houston was a remarkable sight from the conference room wall-to-wall windows.

"No, I don't need anything. Thanks. I'll head on over."

Every step toward the Hobo room was like walking on crushed glass. She didn't know what to expect. Well, that was a lie. She knew exactly what was about to happen. Crystal only wished it wasn't true.

Her father taught her to be strong in the face of adversity. No matter the outcome, she would rise again. And better. She squared her shoulders, took a sharp breath, and strutted into the room like she was untouchable.

"Good morning, everyone." Crystal mustered the cheeriest voice she had.

A round of "good morning" and "welcome back" followed from the eight board members seated in the room. Her parents and her sister Layla occupied four of the board seats. Layla acted as proxy for their sister Ava. The remaining five members were unrelated.

She resisted the urge to squirm under her father's gaze, as she'd been avoiding him since her release from jail. He'd taught her to be strong, and in her defense, that's what she'd been doing by trying to handle this ordeal on her own. Who wanted to run to their daddy every time they got into trouble?

Not Crystal.

The first vice president Rick Fuller—as in full of himself—started the meeting. The lean blond-haired man wore his red power tie and expensive suit today. He'd been itching for the opportunity to become CEO, and it seemed he was dressed for the occasion. This whole meeting was probably his idea. Crystal clamped her teeth to keep a straight face.

"Now that everyone's here, I call this meeting to order at 9:02 a.m. Ms. Langston, as you're aware from the e-mail, we've called this special meeting because you were sent to jail for murdering your ex-husband and the backlash Langston Brands is facing because of it."

"Excuse me, Rick, but I'm innocent, which is why I'm sitting here today. This is something we can come back from," Crystal blurted in a tone higher than intended.

Her pulse raced. Heat gathered at the back of her neck. She'd convinced herself that she'd be able to sit through whatever he was about to say, however, she couldn't. Why would she allow him to crucify her and build his case to take her place?

He shot her one of those agitated I'm-not-finished-talking looks—the look that made her skin crawl. The look that made her inwardly roll her eyes most times.

"While we understand that, we also must think about our shareholders, our buyers, and ultimately our customers. A man was murdered. And not just any man. Your ex-husband and a pro athlete. As CEO, you're the face of this company, and guilty or not, this isn't something that's going away overnight."

Tell me about it.

Crystal nodded, but not because she agreed with him, but because of what no one else besides Marcel knew. Someone was after her. Maybe she should willingly step down. Perhaps that would keep her family out of this and not give Rick another reason to show why he'd be better suited as CEO.

"I understand."

Surprise registered in Rick's eyes, but he recovered quickly. He slid an electronic tablet in her direction and pointed at the screen. "You also understand that in paragraph five point eight of your contract, and I'm paraphrasing, it says that you aren't to bring any negative attention to this company. To put it simply, your personal life can potentially destroy our brand, and we believe it's in the best interest of the company for you to step away for a while."

She didn't bother to look at the screen. Instead, Crystal turned to look at her father.

"How long is a while?"

Rick jumped back in. "At least until you're out of the headlines and the board agrees your presence does more good than harm to Langston Brands."

"I see."

Rick continued, "All those in favor of Ms. Langston's temporary departure from Langston Brands as CEO until the situation has been resolved, raise your hand."

Layla was the only one who didn't raise her hand. That was two votes since she was proxy for Ava. Her mother slipped her hand up and mouthed, *Sorry*. Her father pushed his hand in the air, but she couldn't read his tight-lipped expression. His furrowed brows spoke volumes. Lamont Langston was not happy.

"All who oppose?" Rick asked with a slight glimmer in his eyes. She couldn't help but think he was enjoying this.

Her sisters always had her back, and though Ava wasn't present, Crystal was sure she'd side with Layla. She gave a gentle nod in Layla's direction, but she knew what she needed to do before Rick made the motion.

"I's have it."

Crystal pushed away from the shiny oval mahogany table where she sat at the head.

Rick pressed a button on the conference room telephone to buzz security. Before he could get the words out, her father said, “That isn’t necessary.”

She leaped out of her seat. “I’ll see myself out. Thanks.”

She had to get away before her father forced the conversation she didn’t want to have.

Before her mother offered more apologies.

Before Layla questioned her game plan.

With her head held high, she strutted to the elevator and hit the call button. Maybe she and Marcel could have a late breakfast. Crystal stepped onto the elevator. When the doors were closing, she’d almost called herself safe until a hand reached through the small opening and caused the doors to retract.

Lamont Langston stepped onto the elevator and hit the garage floor button.

“I think it’s time we had a chat.”

Fourteen

It had to be the longest elevator ride she'd taken in her life.

Her father stood next to her. Stoic. Quiet. Eyes straight ahead.

But his towering presence spoke volumes.

Her stomach clenched, and she withdrew to that eight-year-old-girl waiting for her punishment after she'd busted one of the windows out of the front door. She'd already been placed in the proverbial time-out. What was next?

The elevator doors opened at the garage level. When they stepped off, her father placed a comforting hand on her shoulder. Still, he didn't speak. She turned to face him when they arrived at her car and braced herself for what she might see in his eyes.

"You've had quite the weekend. How are you, my dear?"

Crystal cocked her head to the side and raised an eyebrow. She'd expected to hear of his disappointment in her and why she'd even been near Dante in the first place.

"Considering the circumstances, I'm okay, Dad."

He nodded, but rubbed his freshly trimmed beard and squinted as if deciding whether to believe her.

He turned away, stuffed one hand in his pocket, and gestured with the other and paced in front of her. "I want to be clear about why I voted against you back in there. This is business, and my love for you does not interfere with my business decisions. As a result of these unfortunate circumstances, Rick will serve as your temporary replacement."

She couldn't contest that decision, but her skin crawled at the thought. Crystal rubbed her hands along her arms to stave off the inward discomfort manifesting itself.

Her father stopped pacing, turning to face her again, lifting her chin so that their eyes met, and said, "In the meantime, get some rest and focus on you. We need you at your best when it's time for you to come back."

How long will that be? Crystal wanted to ask but knew he wouldn't know the answer to that question without having all the facts. The fact now being that someone was after her. She had to deal with that, and the cops needed to find the real killer before her life could return to normal.

"We're halting the launch of the new collection, right?"

She knew the answer, but needed to hear it.

"Absolutely. We can't launch when the brand image is seen in a negative light—"

"Because of me. It's okay to say it, Dad. My messy personal life put us in this mess."

He placed his hands on her shoulders. "I'm not here to tear you down, my dear. Yes, Langston Brands is facing a little heat from shareholders and buyers right now, but it's all temporary. It's one of those things I warned you about when you first brought up the idea of going public. We have others' interests to consider now. Things will work themselves out. I've been around long enough to understand that. Like I said, take care of you. Let the rest of us handle business here."

Crystal stepped into his arms and squeezed his neck. "I've worked so hard to get here, Dad. I just can't lose it."

"And you won't. This is temporary."

Crystal took a deep breath, inhaling his long-time scent of Creed, and willed herself to pull it together. She wouldn't cry over administrative leave. She'd fix her thoughts on getting the weirdo off her back and preparing for her return to the company.

She stepped out of his arms and pressed the key fob to unlock her car door.

"Thanks, Dad. I guess I'd better go."

He opened her car door, and she slid in.

"I meant what I said. Get some rest. The job will be here when it's time for you to return."

"'Kay."

Crystal started the engine.

Before her father closed the door, he pointed and said, “Your sister is on the way over.”

Seconds later, Layla hopped in the passenger’s seat with their sister Ava on the line on a video call. She turned the phone so that Ava could see Crystal.

“What’s going on out there, Crys?” Ava’s voice rang through the phone.

Crystal shot a warning glance at Layla. “I’m pretty sure Layla has told you everything. No need for me to repeat it.”

“Yeah, I did, but something else is going on, and we want to know what it is,” Layla added. “You walked away too easily.”

Crystal looked into eyes that mirrored her own. It was crazy how looking at the two of them was like looking into a mirror.

How much should she tell them?

And would telling them about the threats put them in danger?

Crystal shook her head and waved her hands to dismiss Layla’s concerns.

“Too easily? It really isn’t anything I can do right now. I believe Rick has a point. When all of this Dante business blows over, I’ll be back. The time off is probably good for me anyway. I was pulling seventy-hour weeks, remember?”

Layla gave her a side-eyed glance. “You’re not going home to sulk over Dante, are you?”

Ava sucked the air between her teeth. "He was her husband. She can cry one time and let it all out."

"Y'all are getting too soft for me because baby, after bruising you up, he's lucky you weren't the one to pull the trigger. You'll always have that scar on your forehead to remind you of his abuse."

"Layla," Crystal and Ava shouted simultaneously.

"What? I'm keeping it real. But anyway, you know I know when you're lying to me. Does this have anything to do with Marcel?"

"No." There went the high-pitched foreign voice again.

Her sisters shot her raised eyebrows. Crystal cleared her throat and answered again.

"Marcel is not involved in what happens at Langston Brands, so no, this has nothing to do with him. He's my friend and my lawyer when it comes to the charges filed against me regarding Dante. There are some other things he's helping me with, and not working for a while can help me clear it up sooner rather than later."

Layla threaded her arms across her chest.

"What things?"

"I promise to tell you all everything when the time is right, but not now. It's for the best." A shiver coursed through Crystal at the thought of the darkness and insanity of the messages she'd received.

She'd shared some truth with them, and that was probably already too much information. Besides, it wasn't much either of them could do.

She and Marcel could handle it.

Ava spoke up. "Crys, keeping us in the dark is not helping the situation. At least tell me and Lay what's going on. This secretive business has to stop. You know I first heard about this craziness from one of the buyers here in London?"

Oh great, the entire world knows about this insanity.

Crystal shoved her head against the headrest.

She dared not ask the buyer's response and whether they had second thoughts about partnering with Langston Brands. Crystal couldn't shoulder one more burden as a result of Dante's murder.

"Trust me, I got this. When have I ever not been able to care for myself? Besides, Marcel is better suited to work with me in this situation. Just give me some time, and I promise to give you more info. Deal?"

Layla tossed her head back against the head rest and bellowed, "Honey, if my belly ain't doin' the Cupid Shuffle right now."

Crystal chuckled and rolled her eyes. "You are so dramatic. I swear you should be starring in somebody's movie."

"But you know Lay has a point. Every time she gets these feelings, something bad happens."

Crystal couldn't disagree there.

Layla warned her before going to the class reunion last Friday, which resulted in one of Crystal's worst nightmares.

"Okay, so what else can I do to give you two assurance?"

Ava said, "Join us on the family tracking app and keep your location turned on so we'll always know where you are, especially since you're on leave for a while. You won't have to worry about us calling you every day to see where you are. We could just check the app."

"I don't understand how knowing my location helps."

"Well, I, for one, would have known you were in jail instead of hearing about it from someone who's not family."

Crystal gave her attention to Ava on the video call. "And what exactly would you have done thousands of miles away?"

Ava held her palm up and leaned away from the screen. "Who knows? But do you have a better idea, Ms. I Can Handle Things Myself?"

"I don't, but what makes you think you need to track me?"

Could they see the fear in her eyes? Hear it in her voice? Was it something about the way she carried herself that alluded something potentially dangerous could be happening?

"Layla has it on her phone. Mom and Dad have it, too. Just a precaution. Anything could happen."

Crystal's expression must have been stuck in a frown because Ava kept trying to convince her.

"You know I watch the ID channel. A lot of horrific things happen to people, and with a simple tracker on your phone, it can help loved ones find you before it's too late. Think of this: You were right there when Dante was shot. How do you know the perp doesn't think you saw them? Maybe they'll come after you, too. It's not farfetched. Crazier things have happened."

"Fine."

Crystal downloaded the app and turned on her location.

Ava somehow figured out some of what was happening without even knowing about the threats Crystal had received. If Crystal said anything about it now, no doubt her sisters would try to help, and that was precisely what Crystal didn't want—her family involved.

She'd clean this mess up herself.

"My belly is feeling better already," Layla said.

Crystal shook her head at Layla's exaggeration. "I'm sure of it."

"Maybe it's because I'm not there, but I'm worried about you, Crys. Just know we're here for you whenever you need us."

"I know. Love you, Ava."

Layla reached over and hugged Crystal. "I'll call you later. Love you."

Ava waved good-bye to her through the video. “Love you, too.”

Layla climbed out of Crystal’s coupe. “Later.”

She’d put an earbud in her ear to continue her conversation with Ava—without Crystal. And frankly, Crystal didn’t like it. She felt out of the loop. Excluded. Perhaps they were experiencing the same feelings, but it had to be this way.

For now.

∞

Marcel nursed his cup of coffee while he waited for Crystal to arrive and join him at the Taste Bar and Kitchen. He’d already secured a patio table so they could talk freely. It also gave him a clear vantage point to see her when she arrived. The light October breeze coupled with the soft sounds of R&B music coming from the restaurant sound system made for a pleasant atmosphere, one where he could enjoy Crystal’s company, even though a serious discussion loomed.

Despite the circumstances, the two of them had easily fallen back into step. Just like old times. He couldn’t recall a time when talking to Crystal about anything had been awkward. They had a natural rhythm. He just hoped they could get through this craziness with the anonymous messages so they could move on and hopefully explore what life could offer them. Together. Why else would he still feel so connected to her after all this time?

He sensed her presence long before she appeared at the outside hostess stand. This indescribable tingle made itself known at the base of his neck. She must have felt his eyes taking in her beauty because she turned to look at him while talking to the hostess. And there was that smile again.

The one he'd seen in his dreams last night.

The one that made him feel like she was happy to see him.

The one that made his heart create a new rhythm. Marcel cleared his throat, waved her over, and stood.

"Hey." Her voice was as sweet as the sugar in his coffee.

He pulled out the chair for her, but instead of sitting, she encircled her arms around him. Crystal squeezed for much longer than he anticipated. With her head snug against his chest, he hoped she couldn't feel the wild beating of his heart. He sensed she must have had a rough morning so he held her until she let go.

Her grip loosened, and Marcel followed suit.

They didn't exchange words. She only looked up at him and smiled before taking her seat.

Were her eyes watery?

She looked away before he could be sure.

Marcel reclaimed his own seat, took a gulp of his coffee, and waited for her to speak.

Crystal peeled her eyes away from the menu and placed it on the table. "Okay, this will be the only time I'll complain about this, but the hold Dante seems to have over my life is unfair. He's not even here anymore, and I'm still tied to him." She leaned closer and tapped her fingers on the table matching every syllable. "As of this morning, I've been temporarily relieved of my duties as CEO of Langston Brands."

"I'm sorry, Crys. Is it because of your arrest?"

"Yeah. I bet this was all Rick's idea, too. He's the first VP, and it's no secret he wants to be CEO."

She folded her arms across her chest. Although she was upset, all he could think about was kissing her pouty lips until she felt better.

Be a better friend.

"What can I do to help?"

"The sooner we figure out who's behind the messages, the sooner I can get my life back. I'm almost sure whoever it is is also the person who killed Dante. It only makes sense."

"I will get in touch with Terry. He sat at the check-in table. We can get a list of everyone who was there. I'll have our investigator do some digging, and we'll see if we can find anyone with possible motive."

The waitress interrupted them with a glass of water for Crystal and to inquire if they were ready to order. Crystal nodded and accepted the glass. She sipped the water. "This could be dangerous, though, and you getting involved even more may impact your career as well. Look at what happened with me. I don't want this situation to hurt your campaign."

"I don't think my campaign will suffer by me helping you. Besides, it'll give us both peace of mind to get this situation straightened out. I think someone may be trying to scare you. If they wanted to harm you, they could've done so already."

The waitress returned. Marcel ordered the pecan praline waffles. Crystal ordered the red velvet waffles. When the waitress whisked away, Crystal reached across the table and wrapped her hands over his. "I really feel like I owe you because this is going out of your way for me, and I'm not quite sure I'm in a place to be asking this of you."

"All you ever need to do is ask, and I'm there. That's always been the case."

Her lips parted, but she didn't respond. Her gaze held his. His arms grew warm. His throat felt drier with each passing second. With their hands still touching, he wondered if it was having the same effect on her as it was on him.

Crystal's eyes shifted, then she slid her hands away and into her lap.

She felt it, too.

Yes.

Crystal cleared her throat. “In other news, Layla senses something else might be happening and that I stepped away from the job too easily.”

“Did you have a choice?”

“Of course not. It was happening either way. I guess she wanted me to put up a useless fight. I didn’t tell my sisters about the note and the text message, but they convinced me to join this family tracking app so they’d know my location at all times.”

Marcel chuckled. “I’m sorry. I know it isn’t funny, but you should see your face. Looking like a teenager upset because she can’t sneak over to her boyfriend’s house anymore.”

Crystal joined him in laughter. “That’s exactly how it feels, but if it makes them happy and keeps them from asking questions, I’ll take it.”

The server returned with their food, interrupting their conversation. Marcel blessed the food. “Dear Lord, thank You for this food and Your blessings. Please bless our food to strengthen our bodies and let no harm come to our bodies because of it. I also ask that You protect Crystal and give her guidance as only You can. In Jesus’ name. Amen.”

After his first bite of pecan praline waffles, he said, “This is dessert, not breakfast.”

“It looks so good. Can I try?”

Marcel pushed his plate in her direction. She cut off a forkful, swirled it in the caramel sauce, and shoved it in her mouth. She moaned with pleasure, and Marcel thought he might lose his mind.

He gulped his coffee again, finishing it off.

"I know Olivia must have some thoughts about your association with me, seeing as though you've just launched your campaign. Did she advise you to stay away from me?"

He wiped his mouth, cleared his throat, and positioned the napkin in his lap.

Thankful they were the only customers who occupied the patio, he could speak freely, though he kept his tone low.

"Actually, Liv thinks me helping you will be good for this campaign."

Her eyebrows bunched together, and he explained further.

"There will be questions about how me helping you get released from jail will influence my campaign and questions about your innocence. She thinks it's best if we get ahead of it and put it all out there. Either way, the questions are coming."

Crystal chewed and thought for a moment, twisting her lips and staring off into space. "I understand."

"You do?"

"I wish I could put this all behind me, but that isn't going to happen. I've heard quite a bit about Liv and how she's gotten other politicians elected. I trust her judgment, and I trust you, too."

That discussion went better than he thought it would. He'd been sure he'd have to convince Crystal to see how this could benefit them both, which would've been difficult because he wasn't entirely convinced. Like her, he just wanted this behind them because this wasn't one of his ordinary criminal cases. It involved someone he cared about; it was personal, and he didn't want to give the crazy person behind the anonymous messages any ammunition.

But he had a sinking feeling in the pit of his belly that's exactly what bringing Crystal into this campaign would do—provide ammo.

Fifteen

Thirty minutes before the town hall's scheduled start time, Marcel networked and mingled with staff members of Texas Southern University's Barbara Jordan–Mickey Leland School of Public Affairs. Dr. Nicholas Thacker, dean of the school, monopolized most of his time. Marcel had to admit that he was flattered by how much Dr. Thacker knew about him and his career. According to him, he made it his business to keep an eye on black lawyers in the area who had the propensity to invoke change.

The older black gentleman smoothed his thumb and forefinger around his goatee. He began nodding, and a gleam lit his eyes. Dr. Thacker shook a finger at Marcel as if an idea had popped in his head.

"You know what, Attorney Singleton, I believe you embody the characteristics of the school's namesake."

"Thank you, sir." Marcel knew Attorney Barbara Jordan's background, but he had a feeling Dr. Thacker was about to give him a brief history lesson.

Dr. Thacker placed a firm hand on Marcel's shoulder.

"You see, Barbara Jordan was a member of the inaugural class here at TSU, was the first Black woman to serve in the Texas Senate and the first black woman from the South to serve in Congress. In 1975, her efforts helped to expand the Voting Rights Act to include minorities. Pretty impressive for a young woman from Fifth Ward with the odds stacked against her."

Marcel nodded, encouraging him to continue.

Students and other faculty members filed into the room, but Marcel gave Dr. Thacker his undivided attention.

When he finished counting off Barbara Jordan's accolades, Dr. Thacker said, "She's paved the way, and I'm honored to support someone in our community who seeks to edify our people and pursue justice. No one should have to pay for a crime they didn't commit, nor should punishment be served unequally because of race. I applaud your tenacity, young man."

"I appreciate the encouragement."

Marcel ended the conversation with a handshake. He waved to a few others already seated in the stadium-style chairs and claimed his seat between Crystal and his sister and campaign manager, Olivia.

Crystal offered an encouraging smile and soft squeeze on his arm.

They didn't exchange words, but the gesture comforted him. To know she chose to be by his side meant the world to him, even if he made a fool of himself this evening. He doubted he would, but in the rare case that happened, Crystal beside him somehow made him feel like everything would be alright no matter what happened.

Jerome Thomas, the student representative for the School of Public Affairs, acknowledged the staff, offered a quick prayer, and gave opening remarks. Afterward, another student, Melanie Woodward, presented a PowerPoint and discussion about the importance of voting. Marcel was impressed by her passion and enthusiasm for the subject. If he weren't a voter, she would've convinced him otherwise.

Dr. Thacker commanded everyone's attention at the front of the room. "We have a bit of a deviation to our scheduled program. DA Sanbridge had to cancel, so we'll extend our question-and-answer period."

"Attorney Marcel Singleton who's launched his campaign for district attorney is here to share his knowledge about the importance of voting and his heart for why he's campaigning for district attorney. Please join me in welcoming him to the stage."

The crowd erupted into applause when Marcel stood. He shook Dr. Thacker's hand and accepted the microphone. Marcel glanced around the room at the faculty, staff, and young, promising faces of TSU's students. An uneasy feeling snaked up his neck when he locked eyes with one man, but Marcel brushed it off to focus on the task at hand.

∞

Entranced by Marcel.

Underneath the muscle, confidence, and heart-captivating smile, wasn't he still the skinny, nerd turned ladies' man she'd called friend all these years? Maybe. But he'd grown into much more than that, and every part of her noticed.

She pressed a hand into her chest and took a slow, deep breath. Not because he'd started talking about ensuring the right people were punished for their crimes, but because she was becoming increasingly aware of him as a man. Not just her friend. And a part of her felt wrong for noticing him that way.

"As many of you are aware, I represent Crystal Langston who was arrested and released in the death of her ex-husband, Dante Green—"

Crystal's ears plugged.

Olivia reached over and squeezed her hand, yet her touch provided little comfort. If her heart had legs, it would have run out of her chest when he mentioned her name. Yes, she'd given him permission to talk about her temporary incarceration—to get in front of things as Olivia put it—and now she wasn't so sure she was ready to put her personal life out there, although it was too late to rescind her agreement, and everyone knew about it anyway.

But still. Facing it in public was a different story.

She'd done press conferences before. Been in the limelight for years. When had a situation like this ever gone well?

She held her breath. And waited.

Waited for the audience to flood Marcel with questions.

Waited for someone to take their chance at ripping her reputation to shreds because they were fans of Dante.

Crystal looked over her shoulder. Her eyes swept the room.

The students sat intently listening, some of them leaning forward in their seats. Others had scrunched eyebrows like they were formulating questions in their mind. The staff members' demeanors were the same. Were they deferring to the students?

Marcel gestured toward the back row. Several people, including Crystal, turned to see who now had the floor.

She couldn't see the man's face clearly because he sat in the back of the room.

"First off, I applaud what you're doing, brother. Second, about this case you mentioned, I seem to remember that the police had solid evidence that Mrs. Green—excuse me, Ms. Langston—shot and killed her ex-husband. We also know she had motive. What kind of black magic do you have that you were able to get the charges dropped?"

Marcel didn't miss a beat.

She could tell he wanted to interject as the man was speaking, but he remained poised and professional. Crystal applauded him for keeping his cool. It was obvious—at least to her—that the man was a fan of Dante. Or he was one of those people who liked to play devil's advocate.

Crystal reminded herself to stay calm.

"As I stated earlier, Ms. Langston's situation is a classic case of ensuring that innocent people don't pay for crimes they didn't commit. The evidence supports my client's innocence. I was there to ensure she was treated fairly and that the system didn't fail her."

"But wasn't she the last person to see him alive?"

Audible gasps filled the room as if added information was presented to them.

Was she on trial?

Accusatory eyes gazed at her, then to Marcel, awaiting his response.

"As you mentioned, my client and the deceased have history, but that does not make her guilty. We've proven that fact, which is why she's able to sit here with us today. That's my promise to any of my clients and to my constituents who chose to elect me as their next district attorney—that they don't serve time for crimes they didn't commit and that they're given an opportunity to prove their innocence. Does anyone else have anything else they'd like to discuss?"

Crystal's heartbeat returned to normal.

Thank You, Lord.

Marcel handled that well.

But she knew this wasn't the end. This situation was far from handled and far from over.

∞

Relief coursed through Marcel at the end of the town hall. He hated bringing Crystal into this or increasing her discomfort, but he'd glanced over at her on more than one occasion, and she seemed to be handling it well.

Including the questions from the man in the back of the room who seemed intent on blaming Crystal for Dante's murder.

He expected inquiries about the closed case, but his questions seemed personal, vindictive even. Marcel had to fight to keep his tone even and voice professional throughout.

He shook hands with the students and staff at the end of the town hall and even stayed behind to network. According to Olivia, he shouldn't run out the door as soon as the event ended, not that he planned to do that anyway, but his mind had been on Crystal. Was she really alright after all that?

Dr. Thacker and the student representative, Jerome, were thc last two left in the room aside from Crystal and Olivia.

Jerome approached him. "Attorney Singleton, I admire what you're doing. I hope you win so that one day I can take your seat and carry the torch. Our generation may not understand just how important your election will be for our community, but I do."

"Thank you, young man, and I look forward to the day you can carry the torch. We need more young people with a passion to change the justice system."

"Oh, trust, there are plenty of us here at TSU. We're tigers, and we have tiger spirit."

Marcel chuckled. "I hear you. When do you graduate?"

"Next year, then I'll apply to law school."

"Here at Thurgood Marshall?"

"That's the plan."

"We'll see about getting Liv to help you on your campaign when it's time."

"Means a lot to have the support of someone like you. Congratulations. We'll hold several voting rallies to make sure we get people registered to vote, and hopefully that means more votes for you."

"Hey, I'll take it. Just let me know if there's anything I can do to help."

Dr. Thacker interjected, "You can bet on it."

Jerome shook Marcel's hand before leaving. Crystal and Olivia joined Marcel's side and shook Dr. Thacker's hand.

"Ms. Singleton, we have you to thank in making sure we got the attorney here tonight, so thank you. And Ms. Langston, I know the conversation got a little heated, but I want to thank you for keeping a good attitude. You could've given that man a piece of your mind or even stood to defend yourself, so thank you for showing our students how to act with tact."

Crystal nodded and accepted his hand. "Thank you, Dr. Thacker."

After a final round of good-byes, they exited the building.

Marcel and Crystal walked Oliva to her car, then they climbed into his vehicle. He pushed the button to start the engine then turned to Crystal.

"I know I've said it a thousand times, but thank you."

This evening turned out better than he imagined. Marcel offered Crystal a smile. He was feeling good about this evening's events—that is until Crystal checked her vibrating phone and showed him the anonymous text.

Marcel can't save you. It won't be long before you get what you deserve.

Sixteen

Crystal's belly sank. Overall, she was feeling good about the town hall and the way Marcel handled the questions. But that message interfered with her sense of peace. She'd blocked the first number, but this text message came from a different one.

How many numbers does this person have?

His voice cut through the silence. "This stuff is getting crazy."

Crystal's heart hammered in her chest.

"Have you talked to Detective Diggins? Was he able to trace the first number?"

"Nah, he couldn't trace it. As we suspected, it was a burner phone."

"And this one probably is, too."

She rested back against the cool leather seat and stared ahead. Nothing to see but the concrete wall in the parking garage. The silence between them didn't bring her any comfort, especially considering Marcel could find anything to talk about. His closed lips made her insides cringe and the tiny hairs along her arms stand.

“We have to find out who’s behind these messages. Do you mind if we skip dinner with Liv, order takeout, and start looking for answers? I want it over.”

“I don’t mind at all. That’s exactly what I think we should do. Let me call Liv.”

Crystal listened to Marcel’s end of the call. He told Olivia that he and Crystal wanted to spend some time alone. With her matchmaking hat on, Olivia didn’t think twice about his decision, nor did she question him. He ended the call with promises to call her the next day.

“Sorry this is ruining your evening.”

“You’re not ruining anything. Let’s just get this out here right now: I’m helping you because I want to, not out of pity. You’re not a burden to me, Crys. Although I hate that it’s under these circumstances, I’m glad we get to spend this time together. We gotta get this taken care of because we don’t know what this person is capable of.”

Crystal forced her mind not to reel from the fact Marcel looked forward to their time together, regardless of the circumstances. She released a soothing breath. This was not a romantic thing. Why would her mind even go there at a time like this?

"You think the guy asking all the questions about me might have something to do with it?"

"The message makes it sound like he's connected."

Crystal propped her elbow on the door and rested her chin on her fist. Her head ached from trying to make sense of the notes and scrubbing through her brain considering who may be responsible and why.

"That's what we're going to find out—my promise to you."

Marcel strapped on his seat belt. "Okay, so what are we doing for dinner then?"

"Chinese. I'll order from my favorite place."

Crystal ordered their dinner online from her phone, then punched the address into Marcel's GPS. Comfort food was what she needed, and egg rolls with combination lo mein called her name. A delicious dinner combined with Marcel's drive to help solve her problems gave her a bit of solace.

But what gave her pause was the idea of spending the next several hours with Marcel.

Alone.

Even though this was business and not at all romantic, her emotions didn't quite get the message. Was she ready for more extended time alone with him?

∞

Marcel led Crystal into his brick one-story, four-bedroom home.

"Alexa, turn on the lights."

The foyer, living room, and kitchen illuminated.

"Fancy smancy."

Marcel chuckled. "Nah, the virtual assistant makes life a little easier since it's just me."

"This is quite a lot of space for just one person. You sure some woman isn't going to jump out of one of those back rooms?"

Marcel threw his head back and laughed. "Definitely not. I've never even allowed a woman to leave a toothbrush over here."

"Commitment issues?"

"Nah. Just haven't been that serious about anyone and don't want to send mixed signals."

"Hard to believe no woman has tried to snatch you up."

"And if I'd allowed a woman to snatch me up, as you put it, I'm pretty sure she'd be just like Dante was back in the day and demand I not spend so much time with you."

Crystal pressed her hands to her chest. "Li'l ol' me?"

"You're a beautiful, successful woman. She might think you'd try and put the moves on me."

It was Crystal's turn to laugh. "I'm as innocent as they come."

"That's too bad."

Crystal's laugh rang through the empty home, filling it with something it'd been void of—someone like her.

"Mind if we eat in front of the fireplace?"

Marcel raised questioning eyebrows. "Are you sure?"

"Yeah. I'm a little chilly, and I could use a bit of relaxation."

"Your wish is my command. I'll grab a few pillows and a blanket."

Marcel flipped the switch to turn on the fireplace then left to find a blanket and pillows. He wasn't necessarily prepared to sit on the floor. In fact, he couldn't recall a time when he ever did so. The fireplace had been used maybe five times in the five years since he owned the house. It was primarily there for aesthetics. He rummaged through his master bedroom closet and pulled out the only other comforter he owned besides the one on his bed.

When he returned to the living room, Crystal was kneeling on the floor going through the food bag. She glanced away from her task and smiled up at him.

"Ready?"

"I hope this is okay. I don't really own many blankets, so this comforter will have to do."

He spread it on the floor and reached for her hand, guiding her to a spot in front of the flames.

"This is perfect." She shimmied her shoulders. "The heat feels so good."

Crystal handed his food container to him, then pulled her own out of the bag. She nodded in his direction, and he took that as his cue to bless the food. She placed the pillow in her lap and propped the container on top. For several bites, they ate in silence. A comfortable silence. A fleeting thought crossed his mind: He could do this over and over again. He shook the thought from his head, suppressed it, and opened conversation to keep his mind on the reason that brought them together.

"A few videos of the mixer have been posted on the class Facebook page. Have you had a chance to look at them?"

Crystal swallowed her food and shook her head. "No, I haven't. What'd you notice?"

"Nothing out of the ordinary, but I think it's a good place to start." He pulled out his phone, opened the videos, and handed the phone to her. "Take a look at these, and tell me if there's anyone you think might have an issue or connection with either you or Dante, you know, aside from the fact that we're classmates."

Marcel ate his dinner while Crystal viewed the five posted videos. She remained quiet while each one played through to the end. Without appearing too creepy, he watched her, waiting for recognition to flash in her eyes or some type of reaction, but there was nothing.

Crystal handed his phone back to him.

"Really, the only person I think has the most connection would be his agent, Jacob. They've been friends for a long time, and although Jacob and I have butted heads a few times over the years, I don't think he'd kill Dante. And these messages don't seem like something he'd do. We've always been cool. He's even called to check on me from time to time since the divorce. I don't think he'd have anything to gain from killing Dante."

"Could be a good place to start digging. Let's talk about Jacob's relationship with you and Dante over the years. Maybe something will come to you."

Crystal stared ahead. Her eyes glazed over as if her thoughts went back in time.

Was he being insensitive? Sure, they were there to try and figure out what was happening, but the look in Crystal's eyes made him wonder if they should wait.

"You sure you want to do this now?"

"What do you mean? Of course I do. That's why I'm here."

Marcel placed his food to the side and slid next to her so that they both faced the fireplace. Their shoulders now touched. He measured his words. "It's only been a few days since Dante's been killed, and I'm a little worried that you're not showing any signs of grief. Let me know if this is too much for you."

He could see the flames dancing in her eyes when she looked up at him. "*Hmmm.* My sisters are a little concerned, too, but the truth is, I grieved for Dante after he abused me." She lifted her bang to show off the scar above her eyebrow, and Marcel's heart constricted in his chest.

"While his death is a tragedy, right now I don't feel much of anything."

Marcel didn't know how to verbally respond to that, so he didn't. Instead, he wrapped an arm around her shoulder, pulled her close to him, and kissed her cheek. A kiss that was meant to be a quick peck of comfort was one that lingered for several seconds. Crystal turned her head toward him and offered her lips.

He hesitated until she lifted her chin, giving him permission to kiss her. Marcel wouldn't let the moment pass. He covered Crystal's lips with his own; his hand slid behind her head, drawing her closer. He savored the softness and the saltiness from the Chinese food. Her lips felt better than he'd imagined. The only reason he pulled away was to come up for air.

He didn't realize he held his breath the entire time.

"I've been wanting to do that for years."

Crystal rubbed her thumb under her bottom lip. "Was it worth the wait?"

"Very much so, but I'm going to put some space between us because I may not be able to stop next time."

Crystal chuckled softly and pressed a hand into her chest. The passion was unmistakable. A kiss long overdue. Had she been waiting as long as him to share a kiss? She released a stream of air. She hadn't expressed her feelings, but the kiss did it for her. They had to get back on track.

Why were they here again?

"When you're ready, tell me about Jacob."

"As long as I can remember—at least since Jacob became Dante's agent—he's always had his back. He's the kind of person you wanted advocating on your behalf. Negotiating the best salary. Endorsements. Time on the field. Always about the spotlight and making sure Dante got the recognition he thought he deserved. There were times when I thought he was over the top. Demanding too much of Dante. Wanting him to be part of everything, you know? Every event, interview, fundraiser, party, or whatever it was, he made sure Dante had some part in it. And it wasn't good for our marriage. Dante would always say that he was building a legacy for us and our children and that period of his life had an expiration date."

When she paused, Marcel said, "And that's where you and Jacob bumped heads?"

"All the time. I was the only one who saw the problem. They werc both all about their paper."

Marcel nodded and waited to see if she'd add anything more.

"So, if anything, Dante was valuable to Jacob. He made money when Dante made money. And seeing as though money was all Jacob really cared about, I can't see why he'd want him dead."

Marcel couldn't see a possible motive for Jacob, but it couldn't hurt looking into his background. Maybe they'd come across something or someone that would help connect the dots. Otherwise, they were back at square one, with no answers, and not an inch closer to finding out who was behind the messages.

And that didn't give Marcel any comfort.

Seventeen

Everything about yesterday evening with Marcel felt right. They still had an emotional connection. Reminded her of old times they'd spent together. Except now they were mature adults with more life experience and no outside relationships to stand in their way.

Marcel's selflessness was doing something to her heart. That had to be it. Would she feel this way if their reunion weekend turned out differently or maybe if she still had her job? That way she'd at least have other things to focus on. Not daydreaming about the kiss over her morning cup of coffee.

Crystal ran her hand around the rim of her coffee mug, remembering how his lips moved slow, like he was savoring the taste of her. He was confident. His lips were firm, but gentle. And though unfortunate circumstances brought them together last night, from that point on, she kept hoping he'd kiss her again.

Oh goodness gracious.

Crystal vacated her spot on the kitchen barstool, trotted into her living room, grabbed her Kindle, and snuggled in her recliner. At least she had time to read.

Before opening her latest romance novel, something in her prompted her to check Jacob's social media profiles. They were friends, but only communicated when he called to check on her after her and Dante's divorce. She scrolled and saw that he'd posted his sentiments about Dante, which she figured he'd do, along with pictures they'd taken together over the years. The most surprising post was a picture of him and the woman she'd seen on the cover of *People* magazine with Dante. The caption read, *Saying goodbye is never easy.*

Their arms were looped together, and they were sitting close. And the longer she stared at the picture, the more she thought their features held similarities—like their high cheekbones and the curve of their noses.

She had time so she clicked around until she found Wynter's profile. Wynter Washington. Her profile was public, so it was easy to snoop. Fashion model. Graduate of Texas Southern University. The tall, slender woman was beautiful and looked like she belonged on magazine covers. Big, bright eyes, full lips, and skin that looked like it had never seen a blemish. And in every picture, her hair was gorgeous. Dante's type.

She'd been so engrossed in the woman's page, she jumped when her doorbell rang. At seven in the morning, it was unusual for her to have any visitors, especially without calling first. Thoughts of the messages she'd received flooded her mind, and she hesitated before looking through the peephole.

She released a pent-up breath when she saw Patrice, her administrative assistant at Langston Brands, standing on her porch with a catalog envelope and a cup of coffee.

"Hey. What's going on, Patrice?" Crystal moved to the side to allow her entry.

"I just thought I'd check on my boss after everything that happened yesterday. I was a bit worried and needed to check on you myself."

"I appreciate that, but as you can see, I'm all good."

"Yep. Hair bonnet, lounge pants, and all. I don't think I've ever seen you so relaxed."

Crystal chuckled. "As you shouldn't. Like you said, I'm your boss."

"Right. Speaking of, I also came to bring you your favorite cup of coffee, a skinny vanilla latte," Patrice said and smiled wide, obviously proud of herself for doing so. "And this envelope that arrived at the office for you yesterday."

"Thanks, Patrice. You know I can't grant you any time off for special favors."

Patrice waved her off. "No biggie. It's the least I can do. I know you're going through a tough time, and I'm sure you didn't want to come into the office for this. Plus, it's from a law office, so I wasn't sure if you'd want me to give it to Layla. Seems like it might be personal. It doesn't have Langston Brands or your title on it, just your name."

"Well, in that case, good looking out." Crystal placed the cup on the coffee table and flipped the featherweight envelope over to see the Law Offices of Harley & Hudson, LLP printed on the front. She scrunched her eyebrows, thinking of reasons why she'd receive anything from the law office Dante used for his legal affairs. Curiosity gnawed at her gut.

Patrice backed toward the door. "Well, I need to run so I can make it on time this morning. I know you're out for a while, but please let me know if you need anything, and I'll take care of it."

"I'll do that. Thanks."

When Patrice left, Crystal locked the door behind her and ripped open the envelope.

Lord, please don't let this be anything crazy. I can't take much more.

Crystal read and reread the letter at least three times. Her hands trembled more with each reading.

As the executor of Dante's estate, Gregory Harley's letter notified Crystal that Dante's estate and assets now belonged to her.

He'd file an executor's deed to transfer the Houston real estate to her name immediately.

∞

Marcel's instincts rarely led him in the wrong direction.

He couldn't shake the feeling that Dante's agent, Jacob, deserved a closer look. Though Crystal believed he was incapable of killing Dante or being behind the threats, Marcel didn't give him the benefit of doubt. He'd represented enough criminal cases over the years to know people hid their agendas, and the very person the victim trusted was often the one who'd done them harm.

He hadn't slept well after he took Crystal home last night. Worry kept him awake, but so did his increasing feelings for her. He spent most of his should-have-been-asleep time lying in bed and staring at the ceiling for answers.

When they got through this ordeal, where would that leave him and Crystal? They couldn't go back to not speaking. Couldn't go back to the way things were before their reunion weekend. Or before the kiss.

Did she see him as more than a friend?

She had to—friends didn't share a kiss like they had.

He wanted more than friendship. Did she? Was she ready?

Possible motives Jacob could have for killing his friend—and this was where he came up short. Jacob couldn't benefit from Dante's death.

Marcel went into the office much earlier this morning. Typically, he was a late starter—around nine thirty. But this morning, powered with a mug of caffeine and three hours of sleep, he strolled in at seven to get a jump on his Jacob theory.

Marcel buzzed their office's private investigator, Naima. If anyone could find out information, it was her.

Naima strode into his office wearing all black, as she often did.

"What can I do for you, Mr. Singleton?" Born and raised in Seattle, Washington, he wasn't sure where she picked up the southern accent.

"Mind closing the door?"

He had to limit the details of this case to those on a need-to-know basis. For all he knew, someone in the office could be trying to sabotage his political campaign. Though he believed that to be unlikely, he believed one could never be too careful.

Naima shut the door and claimed a seat in one of the visitor's chairs across from his desk, crossing her legs at the knees. She gestured to him with the wave of her hands and whipped out her phone to take notes.

"Whatcha got for me?"

Always straight to the point. One of the things he liked about her.

"I need you to investigate the background of Jacob Jackson. Jacob is the former agent of the late NFL star Dante Green. Lives in the Houston area. About forty-two years old." Recalling the social media photo Crystal sent to him that morning, he added, "Possible associate, Wynter Washington."

Naima nodded and tapped her notes into the phone. When she finished, she casted a doubtful glance at him. He could see the uncertainty flash in her eyes.

"Yes. This has to do with Crystal Langston."

She hesitated before asking, "Haven't the charges against her been dropped?"

He trusted Naima, so he said, "You're right. The charges were dropped, but she's been receiving threats, and I'm concerned her life may be in danger. Jacob and the deceased were close, so I'm not sure he'd harm him, but I don't think it could hurt to explore all possibilities. There could be something in his background that could give us some insight though. I want to know about his relationship with Dante, his financials, and other known associates, including who he's dating."

"Anything else?"

"That's it for now."

Naima stood. "I'll get started right away and keep you posted."

"Thanks, Naima."

She strutted to the door and swung it open, but didn't leave.

"Oh, hi." Naima moved to the side, and Marcel looked up to see Crystal standing in the doorway poised to knock. Though happy to see her, her wide eyes and lack of a smile told him something was wrong.

Marcel stood, and Naima pulled the door open farther for Crystal to enter. She'd raised questioning eyebrows at Marcel, but didn't say anything. When Naima stepped out of his office and closed the door behind her, Crystal rushed into his arms and squeezed. She was happy to see him. Or scared.

She pulled away, tossed an envelope onto his desk, and thrust her phone in his line of vision.

You're a fool if you think I'm going to let you keep what's mine.

Eighteen

Someone had to be watching her, and that gave her the creeps.

The only thing that text could be referring to was Dante's estate.

But who would believe they had a claim to it? And how would they know she'd receive it?

When Crystal received the anonymous message, she put on proper clothes and headed to Marcel's office. Layla called on the way. Crystal figured she'd had one of her premonitions or something because she always seemed to know when something was wrong. However, she ended the call after five minutes. Anything longer, and she would've let something slip. The most information she gave Layla was about the letter from the lawyer's officc and that she was on her way to visit Marcel to discuss. Though he was a criminal attorney and not an estate attorney, it wasn't illogical to believe that he didn't have some knowledgc about the subject matter.

The latest message had her looking over her shoulder when she climbed out of the car and speed walked through the parking garage to get into Marcel's office building. Upon entry, the receptionist recognized her and gave her permission to walk back to his office. Had Marcel shared anything about their issue with his office? She thought it strange the older, blond-haired woman didn't at least call him first.

Dressed in black like a ninja, a woman swung open his office door as Crystal lifted her hand to knock. And for a sliver of a second, jealousy sliced through Crystal's core. The woman stood about five inches taller than her. Her long, jet-black hair was pulled back into a ponytail and accented her eyes, which were the size and color of almonds, and smooth chocolate skin. A quick, toothless smile graced her features before she moved to the side to allow her entry into Marcel's office. She'd exchanged a look with Marcel before leaving.

Crystal didn't like it, but now wasn't the time for jealousy. Marcel stood, and she rushed into his arms. For the first time since receiving the anonymous text, she felt safe. Lately, he'd become just that to her—her safe place.

Another feeling rose within her. Warmth. An erratic heartbeat. A want-to-be-in-his-arms-for-all-time romantic kind of feeling. And memories of the kiss came flooding back.

She stepped out of his embrace and turned away for a moment to compose herself, to make sure her eyes didn't give away what she was trying to stop her heart from feeling.

Marcel's heavy breath cut through her thoughts.

"Do you have any idea what that message is alluding to? What do you have?"

Crystal sat and blew a stream of warm air through her clenched teeth. She pointed to the envelope her assistant Patrice brought by her house, which she'd dropped on Marcel's desk. "Dante's estate."

Marcel reclaimed his seat and peeled open the envelope. Like her, he must have read the document at least three times before saying anything.

"Wow." He dropped the letter on the desk and locked eyes with her. "If there's someone out there who believes they have a claim to Dante's estate, I can see how they'd be upset. However, the probate court must have determined that the will is valid, which is why the executor has contacted you. There's nothing anyone can do about it at this point."

"I don't care about the house or the money. I just want to be free from all things Dante Green."

"Can you think of anyone who might be interested in his estate?"

Crystal thought for a moment. "Not really. His mom passed away about a year before our divorce. His father was never in the picture, and he doesn't have any brothers, sisters, or children that I know of."

Marcel rubbed his chin, and something flashed within his gaze. That same look he had last night. He was withholding information.

"What is it?"

"In the spirit of transparency, Naima, the woman who was in my office when you got here, is our office's private investigator. She's looking into Jacob for me. I know you don't think he's capable of harming you or Dante, but at the very least, I believe there may be information in his background that could help us."

An idea crept into her mind, one she didn't like, but it was probably their best option at this point.

"Maybe it's time I give him a call."

Crystal hadn't talked to Jacob in a couple of months. The last time they spoke, he'd called to see how she was doing and if there was anything he could do for her. He'd always been like Dante's fix-it man. Even when she landed in the hospital after Dante hit her hard enough for her head to slam against the kitchen island, Jacob came to the hospital to check on her. In fact, it had been him at her bedside when she regained consciousness, not Dante. The more she thought about it, he'd probably only been there in his and Dante's best interest, to ensure she wouldn't press charges and to protect Dante's image.

She dug her phone from her purse and swiped and tapped until she pulled up his contact information. Crystal called with her phone on speaker.

"Crystal, I'm a little surprised to see your number pop up on my phone. You good?"

Thinking back to how he continued to support Dante even in his wrongdoing made her cringe.

She feigned niceties. "I'm doing okay considering everything that's happened. How are you holding up?"

"It's been rough, but I'm making it. I'm leaving to go out of town tomorrow. Think you can have lunch today?"

She glanced at Marcel before answering, "Actually that's perfect."

"Cool. I'll text you the location in a minute. How does eleven sound?"

"Sounds good."

"Okay. See you in a bit."

∞

Marcel and Crystal arrived at the Toasted Yolk about twenty minutes early. There was no way he'd sit back while Crystal went to meet with Jacob alone. Marcel wanted the opportunity to see Jacob's every move from the second he arrived.

They both ordered coffee. When the waitress brought the carafe, Marcel poured both of their cups. Crystal added creamer, stirred, then took her first sip.

"I've probably said this a thousand times already, but thank you. I feel like you've been putting your life on hold to help me deal with this."

"And a thousand times, you're welcome. Don't worry too much about me. I can handle my caseload. I have associates on my team to help when needed, and that's pretty much understood now that I'm running for DA."

Marcel sipped his coffee. He glanced at the entrance every time there was any movement. His seat faced the door so he could watch for Jacob.

"So what I'm hearing is that you're the boss, and you can do whatever you want to do."

Marcel chuckled. He locked eyes with her. "No. What you're hearing is that I'd do anything for you. It's always been that way." He sipped his coffee again before adding, "Just like I let you use me back in junior high to make your li'l boyfriend Chris jealous. Or drive you to the mall every weekend when I first got my driver's license. And follow you to Houston University."

Crystal's eyes grew large. "You're lying. You received your acceptance letter before I got mine."

"True, but Jackson State was first on my list."

Crystal laughed. When she recovered, her smirk remained intact. "What am I going to do with you?"

"I think you know the answer to that already." Marcel held her gaze. They needed to have a conversation about where they were headed because they'd already crossed the friend line. He tore his gaze away and glanced toward the entrance. Jacob walked in. "But that's a conversation for another day." He nodded toward the hostess stand. "Our company is here."

Crystal turned in her seat. Jacob's eyes locked in on hers with a look that made Marcel uncomfortable and ready to protect Crystal if and when necessary against this guy.

Jacob strolled toward their table. His smile grew like he was about to greet an old friend. Crystal didn't stand to greet him, so he leaned over to give her a one-armed hug.

He sat next to Crystal.

Jacob said, "Crys, I'm glad to see you're doing well and to know that the cops didn't find you responsible for my friend's murder."

Crystal frowned. "You know I wouldn't do anything like that."

Jacob picked up the menu and focused on the laminated sheet. "That's what I thought—but I can't say I didn't have my doubts when I found out you were the last one to see him alive."

Crystal turned to face him and propped an elbow on the table. She looked at Jacob like he'd grown another pair of eyes. "But you also know me. I'm surprised you'd think for a second that I'd kill him."

"Relax. I was just stating facts. I don't think you have the guts to commit murder, but not seeing at you at his funeral yesterday made me a little suspicious."

"I didn't need to be there to pay my respects."

Jacob's slow nod and downturned lips spoke volumes. "Do you have any idea who would want my homeboy dead?"

"I was going to ask you the same thing. You knew him better than I did."

Marcel didn't have a solid reason for why something didn't sit right when it came to Jacob. But this conversation wasn't getting them anywhere or providing any information he didn't already have.

"Did Dante have any enemies? Mess around with any married women whose husband's might want revenge?" Marcel asked.

Jacob clasped his hands, rested them on the table, and leaned forward, sporting a crooked smile. "Well, if it isn't Mr. DA."

Jacob hadn't acknowledged Marcel before this point. His patience was on a short string for the man.

"Nah, D wasn't that king of man. Lately, all he talked about was getting his wife back." He maintained eye contact with Marcel and jutted his thumb toward Crystal. “She’s part of the reason he wanted to leave the league. Against my advice, he was ready to retire and work on his marriage.”

Crystal’s expression remained flat.

Zero emotion.

The waitress stopped by to take their orders, but they declined and asked for more time.

“Can you think of anything else that may have seemed off with him before the reunion? Anything that concerned you about him?” Marcel asked.

“What’s with the third degree? Crystal was released, so why are you even concerned with his murder? Are you trying to use this to make yourself look good in your run for DA?”

Jacob had a point there. If Marcel were him, he’d wonder the purpose of the questions, too. Crystal’s release from prison was public knowledge. As her attorney, it would seem he’d move on.

Crystal jumped in. “I’d just like to know what really happened to Dante, especially since I was accused of murdering him. If you were in my shoes, wouldn’t you want to know, too?”

“I guess. But if you want my advice, Crys, I think you should just move on with your life. My friend is gone, and he ain’t coming back. The cops released you from jail. It seems you’re free to do whatever you want. Let the cops worry about what happened to him. Whoever did this will get what’s coming to them.”

"You seem confident in the cops to do their job," Crystal said, her voice doubtful, probably because she was the first person arrested in Dante's murder.

"I have Detective Diggins on speed dial. He'll get tired of me calling and asking for updates."

"Will you let me know if you find out anything?"

Jacob flipped his wrist to check the time. "I will, but listen, I gotta run. I won't be able to stay to eat. There's someone else I need to meet up with before I leave town." He stood and touched Crystal's shoulder. "Take care."

He tossed over his shoulder, "You, too, Mr. DA."

Crystal looked over her shoulder and watched Jacob walk out of the restaurant. She then turned her attention back to Marcel. "I believe he knows something, and he won't share it with me if you're around."

"I hope you aren't thinking about meeting with him by yourself. I still don't trust him."

Crystal sipped her coffee and shrugged. "I'd be perfectly fine if I never talked to him again."

"Good."

Marcel could tell Crystal had at least thought about meeting with Jacob. She wanted answers too bad not to consider it, but Marcel didn't get a good vibe from Jacob. Marcel felt like he was trying too hard. He didn't doubt Jacob wanted justice for Dante, but he didn't buy the fact that Jacob knew nothing. As close as he and Dante appeared to be, there had to be some information he could provide. But maybe Jacob felt the same way about him, that he couldn't trust him.

When the waitress returned again, they both ordered The Works Omelet with a pancake to share. Hopefully, Naima could find something that would give steam to his theory about Jacob. In the meantime, he'd use all this investigation time as an avenue to spend every moment he could get with Crystal.

They'd find out who was behind the messages, which would likely lead them to the murderer soon. His instinct told him they were getting closer.

He watched Crystal check her vibrating phone. She flipped the phone in his direction to read the message.

Don't stick your nose where it doesn't belong. Back off.

Nineteen

A week later, Marcel woke up to four missed calls from Crystal and six missed calls from his sister and campaign manager, Olivia. His stomach dipped. Whatever it was couldn't be good.

He didn't consider himself a heavy sleeper, so he wasn't sure how he slept through ten missed calls.

Issues with his campaign flooded his forethoughts, so he pressed his Bluetooth earbud into his ear and called Olivia first.

"Conspiracy to murder? What in the world is going on with you and Crystal?" Olivia's high-pitched hysterical voice pierced his eardrum. He removed it until she stopped talking.

"Hold up. Hold up. Slow down. Murder? What are you talking about?"

"Check your messages."

Marcel opened his messages. Olivia and Crystal both sent him articles circulating on social media and tabloids containing pictures of him and Crystal holding hands walking out of the restaurant last week and another picture of him kissing her before he opened her car door. The headlines that accompanied the photos were insane.

Lovers Kill Former NFL Player for Money?

And *Scorned Ex-Wife and New Lover Murdered Dante Green.*

And the one that made his blood boil the most, *Killer Fit to Be DA?*

Marcel ran an open palm over his face to relieve the fogginess. This had to be a twisted dream. What was going on?

"I don't know what any of this is about or where these lies are coming from, but you know neither one of us murdered Dante."

"Of course, I know that, and what I also know is that this is fuel for your opponent."

Marcel threw his head back and huffed. He didn't think sitting DA Elliot Sanbridge would fight dirty, or at least spread vicious lies.

This was one nightmare that had no ending.

"I know." Marcel blew a stream of air. "Schedule a press conference. I hate to spend my time even addressing such foolishness, but this has to be done."

"Way ahead of you."

"Thanks, Liv."

"*Ummm-hmmm.* You're welcome. I've worked on a lot of campaigns, but none of my clients have ever been accused of murder. You have something you need to tell me about what's going on with you and Crystal?"

Obviously, whoever was behind this wanted to push his buttons. He was unsure if all this was more about him or Crystal at this point. Crystal had already lost her position at Langston Brands. Did they want to see him lose his position at the law office, too? Pull out of the DA race?

Jacob's image surfaced in his mind. This couldn't be a coincidence. Did he sell the photos and the story to the media so Marcel would shift his focus from looking into Dante's murder? As he thought about it, Marcel grew more suspicious.

"It's a little complicated, and I don't want to involve you in this right now. We can talk about it later when we get this straightened out."

"For the record, I don't like this, Marcel. I don't know what's going on with you and Crystal, but you didn't have these problems until she came back in your life. I like Crystal, I do, but think about distancing yourself from her for a while. This is getting out of hand."

"None of this is her fault, Liv. I've got it under control."

Marcel wrapped up his call with Olivia after that. This little stunt would not define what he would and wouldn't do, nor who he should or shouldn't spend time with. Despite dealing with investigating the threats, he'd enjoyed his time with Crystal. They'd spent every evening together for the past week, with dinner plans tonight. But he had to have this press conference first.

Naima was still doing her part. Like him, she had her suspicions about Jacob, but nothing concrete yet. Marcel tapped and swiped his phone to call her, but his actions were interrupted with a call from Detective Diggins.

"Detective, good morning. What can I do for you?" Marcel paced his bedroom floor. The cushioned carpet comforted him. That call from Olivia, coupled with the detective's call, assured him it would be a long day. He sucked in his breath and prepared for what Detective Diggins had to say.

"Who'd you piss off?"

Marcel imagined his reference had to do with the headlines he and Olivia had just spoken about, but he asked anyway. "What do you mean?"

"Why is your name circulating around my office with the theory you and Ms. Langston conspired to kill Mr. Green?"

Marcel stopped pacing and stood in the center of the room, prepared to defend himself. "Look, detective—"

"Attorney, I know you're not responsible for Green's death, so it makes me wonder what you're stirring up around there. You're doing something that someone doesn't like."

Now he had his attention.

"I'm pretty sure that whoever is behind this fake news is the same person behind the anonymous messages Crystal received."

"Yeah, those. An untraceable burner. All of them. So no leads there."

"And have you looked into Jacob Jackson's background?"

So far, he still didn't have much to go on but instinct, and he'd wager Jacob knew something.

"We've considered him, but so far nothing has come up. Besides, he had an alibi the night Green was murdered. Wynter Washington confirmed that the two of them were together. There were eyewitnesses who also confirmed that he left the area with Wynter after Green's retirement announcement."

Marcel trotted into the kitchen to brew himself a cup of coffee. That wasn't enough to convince Marcel. "While that may be true, he has motive, money."

"Okay," the detective dragged the word out, like he was in deep thought, "but as Mr. Green's agent, that doesn't seem like it would be a problem."

"True, but…" Marcel voiced his theory, "what if money is the issue here? Maybe Dante owed Jacob something, or what if they fought about Dante's retirement plans?" Marcel felt like he was grasping at straws, but he had nothing else on the man yet.

"I'm listening."

"Dante made this announcement at the reunion that he was retiring from the NFL to get Crystal back. Maybe it's not a coincidence that he died following the announcement. Retirement means no need for Jacob anymore and a lot less money lining his pockets."

"Okay, but I'm sure he has other clients."

"None as big as Dante." That was the one piece of information Naima brought back to him that he found helpful and gave steam to his theory.

"That's quite a long shot you have there, but worth digging into. We'll check it out. In the meantime, you and Ms. Langston need to stay under the radar and let us do our job."

∞

Crystal silenced the ringer when Marcel's name appeared on the screen.

After two back-to-back calls, she knew the reason for his calls—the conspiracy theory that summoned Layla to her house this morning. They needed a game plan fast because they hadn't gathered enough information to get them any closer than they were to finding out the truth than they had been a week ago.

If only she could get Layla out of her house quickly without drawing further suspicion, she could get back to Marcel. Layla was the one who got wind of the headlines first from some gossip website. She sent the articles to Crystal and Ava in a group text and announced she was on her way to Crystal's house. Ava asked to be on video call. This ordeal seemed like something she and Marcel needed to work out, not the Langston sister trio. It's not like they could do anything more than her and Marcel.

"What's going on, Crys? You've already been exonerated from this case. Why are you back in the headlines again?" Layla fired her questions first.

They gathered around her coffee table sipping lattes Layla had whipped up in Crystal's kitchen. Layla positioned her phone on the table so that Ava could see them on her phone's camera.

"And with Marcel for that matter?" Ava added from the video call. "Something is going on, and I want the whole story—now."

"There really is no story. I don't know what's happening besides the fact someone is obviously trying to frame me." Crystal threw her hands up. "Why? Who knows?" *Because someone is getting nervous. Maybe we're getting close to the truth.*

It's the only thing that made sense.

Ava folded her arms across her chest and cocked her head to the side with a raised eyebrow. "I think there's more going on than you're telling us, and we can't help you if you don't let us."

Crystal was the oldest. The strong one. The leader. The example. Eyes similar to her own stared back at her. For a second, she considered telling them about the first note left in her hotel room and almost getting run off the road, but then, the inquiries wouldn't end there. This would turn into an even bigger mess with too many people involved. No, she and Marcel needed a little while longer to figure this thing out.

For the next fifteen minutes, they went through the same merry-go-round of question and answers. Layla and Ava wanted to know why someone would still be attempting to set her up and why they'd included Marcel, and Crystal couldn't answer their questions.

Her phone rang again. Thankful for the reprieve, she answered.

"I hate this man is still causing trouble for you."

Lamont Langston, their father.

Crystal's breath caught.

What would he say about all of this?

"Morning, Dad. Looks like the fake news is traveling fast."

"It most certainly is, but my primary concern is you. How are you, my dear?"

"I'm okay, considering everything happening. Don't worry about me."

She surely couldn't mention the anonymous threats to her dad. He'd put a security detail on her, and that was too much, in her opinion.

"I'm your father. It's my job to worry about you. And Marcel, what's he got to do with all this? Something going on with you two I don't know about?"

Though she didn't have the phone set to speaker, her father's voice carried. Before she looked up, Crystal could feel Layla and Ava's eyes burning holes through her skull. Did they think she'd give their father any more information than she'd already given them? She shook her head.

"Dad, there's nothing going on."

Aside from us crossing the line from friends to more than friends. They hadn't discussed that yet.

"Lay and Ava are here with me. We just finished talking about this. Marcel and I will handle it. Just do me a favor and assure the board this is slander. I'm coming back for my job when all this is over. We don't want Rick getting too comfortable."

Her father finally laughed. "He's a good temporary replacement."

Key word being *temporary*.

"Just make sure he knows his days are numbered."

Her father sobered. "Since you've appointed Marcel as the man in charge of your legal needs, I need him to handle this situation ASAP. This is the last time I want your name in the headlines when it comes to this distraction."

"You and me both."

"Take care, and I'll call you this evening."

"Bye, Dad."

Crystal ended the call, threw her head back against the sofa, and released a long stream of air. She couldn't believe how much her life had changed since attending the reunion that dreadful weekend.

The doorbell sounded throughout the house. Crystal leaped out of her seat to see who the visitor could be. Another distraction to keep her from Ava and Layla's impatient stares. She stood on her tiptoes to look through the peephole.

Marcel.

Crystal unlocked the door and swung it open. Marcel kissed her lips, then pulled her into his arms. His firm, yet tender hold around her waist and woodsy scent pacified her.

"Thank God you're okay. I was so worried when you didn't answer your phone. There's no telling what's—"

He stopped and released her.

"Hey, Layla."

"Hey to you, too," Layla said. "Well, there's one thing the headlines got right. When did you two start kissing?"

Ava shouted from the phone. "Who's kissing?"

"Crystal and Marcel. Honey, you should've seen the way he laid one on her."

"It only took him forever," Ava said.

"Ummm-hmmm," Layla said. "We can address whatever is going on between y'all later."

Layla patted the seat next to her in front of her phone's camera. "Come sit down."

Marcel trudged through the foyer and into the living room, accepting the seat Layla offered. Crystal claimed the recliner seat. Layla wasted no time with her round of questions.

Marcel kept his eyes on Crystal while he addressed Ava and Layla's concerns. She sensed there was something else he wanted to share, but not in front of her sisters, at her previous request.

"I wish I had more information. It seems like someone is trying to sabotage my campaign, but I'm not sure why they would bring Crystal into it. I'm going to address the situation in a press conference later this afternoon. The firm's P.I. is also looking into it."

Layla cocked her head to the side and glared at Marcel. "Y'all better work fast. You know how our father is. He just told Crystal that since you've appointed yourself as the person in charge of her legal needs, you need to handle this ASAP. He doesn't want her name in the headlines anymore when it comes to this."

Crystal knew his voice carried, but was surprised Layla specifically heard what their father said. "Dang, girl. You hear everything, don't you?"

"I gotta ear hustle when I'm not getting the whole story." Layla looked between Crystal and Marcel and wagged her finger. "I want the 4-1-1 on what's going on with y'all. How'd I miss this thing y'all have going on?"

Crystal stood. "Can you all give me and Marcel some time to talk? I promise to call y'all later, and let's not forget you can track my every move." Crystal waved her phone in the air.

After engaging in a stare down for what seemed like an eternity, Layla agreed to leave. Crystal walked her to the door. Before leaving, Layla stopped and said to Marcel, "I don't like where any of this is going. Obviously, there are secrets between the two of you, and I trust you because I've known you as long as I have any memories, so promise me that you won't let anything happen to my sister."

"You have my word. I've got Crys."

And Crystal knew he meant it. She felt the sentiment in her bones. Maybe it was the sincerity in his eyes or the way his voice deepened when he said it, or maybe the actions he'd shown since they reconnected. Whatever the case, she believed him, and she trusted him.

When she saw Layla out and closed the door behind her, her phone vibrated in her hand. She flipped it over to check the message.

If you don't give me what's mine, Mr. Future DA won't be able to save you. Neither can that pretty sister of yours.

Twenty

"I can't stay here." Crystal's voice shook, and her hands trembled. She moved across the room like she was looking for something, but never found it.

In four swift steps, Marcel advanced across the floor and stilled her with his hands placed firmly around her arms. "What happened?"

"I think someone is watching me. I can't stay here."

Tears filled her eyes, which tore Marcel's heart in two. He wrapped her in his arms until she calmed.

Crystal stepped out of his embrace and picked up her phone. She tapped the side key to illuminate the screen and showed him the message.

He tensed. Someone was playing a dangerous game, and he vowed to fix it, even if it was the last thing he did.

"You're right. You can't stay here. Pack a bag. You're coming with me."

Crystal pulled her phone to her chest and stared at him. Uncertainty lit her eyes like a toddler hesitant of taking his first step.

"You sure?"

"I am. I have three empty bedrooms in my house. You can even have the master if that's what you want, but I'm not comfortable with you staying here. Plus, I just promised Layla that I'd take care of you. It's a little hard for me to do that with you here and I'm across town. And I think it's clear someone is watching your house—or wants you to believe they are. Either way, I'll feel better with you close to me until we can figure this out."

She nodded, turned on her heel, and disappeared out the room.

He released a breath he didn't realize he was holding. Having Crystal move into his house temporarily was the best course of action in this instance, right? Or would it blur the lines of their whatever-ship even more? They were no longer only friends, but they hadn't established the status of their relationship either.

Twenty minutes later, Crystal returned to the living room with two rolling suitcases. Marcel advanced to her side and grabbed the handles.

"Is there anything else you need to grab before we leave?"

Crystal glanced around the room and shrugged. "No. I'll be okay for a few days."

A few days?

Why did his heart plummet at those words when he knew this arrangement wasn't permanent?

∞

How on earth did one weekend wreck her life?

This was supposed to be the week Langston Brands released their newest handbag collection. A design team she'd been a part of. Not the typical CEO duties, but as a woman who owned a handbag for every occasion and then some, she couldn't help being involved in the process.

She should've been celebrating this entire week. Not going into hiding because some weirdo thought it was a clever idea to send her threats and possibly stalk her.

Marcel's master bedroom was the most desirable, but she couldn't impose on him and allow him to sleep in a guest room in his own house even though he said it was okay. It was a huge leap for her to accept his offer to stay in his home anyway. That was enough taking. Never mind their unspoken romantic interest in each other and the fact she'd practically known him all her life, this felt like too much.

She chose the bedroom farthest away from his and unpacked some of her clothes to hang in the closest. Her toiletries were also put away. Before going out to talk with him, Crystal sat on the bed to decompress. Steady, long, deep breaths.

Her phone vibrated and lit up. After all the crazy messages she'd received, and blocking every number, she was almost afraid to check it, but then she remembered she needed to check in with her sisters. Although they could track her location, she thought it best to clarify why she was staying with Marcel.

Crystal recovered her phone from her purse. She released a deep, relaxing sigh when the notification was a group text from her sisters.

L: I want to know what's going on with you and Marcel. When did y'all start kissing each other? Are y'all dating now? Spill the beans.

She ignored Layla's message.

C: Staying in Marcel's guest room for a few days while we work to put an end to the fake news.

L: And that means you have to move in with him? So you are dating him.

A: Right. Seems that way, Lay. Took him long enough to make his move. Thought he would've done it pre-Dante.

C: Talk to y'all later.

Layla and Ava's messages didn't stop, but Crystal was done. If she were either of them, she'd have questions, too. A fake news story about the two of them scheming to commit murder wasn't enough for her to move in with Marcel. Even she knew that didn't justify the arrangement, but she wasn't going into details right now about the situation or about what was happening with her and Marcel.

All they really needed to know was that she was safe.

Crystal stuffed her phone back into her purse and marched out of her temporary room to meet Marcel in the living room. He sat in front of the fireplace on top of that same comforter they used during dinner. When she walked into the room, he stood and extended his hand toward her. Crystal accepted it, and warmth slid up her arm, through her body, and down to her feet.

Even amid the craziness and all the things wrong around them, she'd found something that felt so right.

Being with him.

∞

Marcel remembered how much Crystal liked sitting in front of the fireplace, so he turned it on to help her relax. He also turned on his Bluetooth speaker to play soft, old-school R&B, just so that it wouldn't be too quiet. 112's "Crazy Over You" hummed through the speakers. He thought to change the song because he wasn't implying anything, but it did fit what was happening in his heart.

When she entered the room, it was as if she'd given his heart a new purpose to beat. When their hands touched, for a moment, he forgot why they were there in the first place, only remembering that having her in his space, in his life, was what had been missing.

But now wasn't the time for that talk.

When would be the right time?

He'd missed out on his chance years ago. He just prayed he got the opportunity when this was over. Marcel didn't want Crystal to think he was taking advantage of their situation, but wasn't there a saying that opportunity rarely knocked twice? He shook his head. Marcel didn't subscribe to that theory. Crystal wouldn't be back in his life again if it weren't meant for them to have a second chance.

He cleared his throat and helped her lower to the blanket before making himself comfortable.

"Here." He reached behind him and grabbed a mug of coffee. "Figured you might want this. Let me know if you get too warm with the coffee and the fireplace going."

She accepted it and cocked her head to the side for a moment. He wanted badly to ask her what she was thinking, mostly because he hoped it was about him. But this wasn't their moment.

"So thoughtful. Thank you." She sipped it. "And perfect amount of added creamer. Someone's been paying attention."

"Always." He sipped his own and waited a beat before he opened the conversation. "So, here's what I'm thinking: Obviously I'm not working today. I'm going to work on my statement for the press conference Liv scheduled for this afternoon. Are you planning to come or stick around here?"

"I feel like you put more emphasis on me staying here."

He sipped his coffee again and measured his words.

"It's not that I don't want you at the press conference, but I think I'll feel better if you stayed. This is a gated community, and the officers are good about monitoring who comes in and out."

He gave himself a silent reminder to stop at the gate and give the officer Jacob's name for the do-not-enter list.

"Besides, we don't know if this person planted this information because they knew I'd hold a press conference so that they can try something there. There are too many unknowns, and I don't like it."

She reached over and squeezed his free hand. "I understand, but I also want to show my face to support you. You've been so good to me. Let me return the favor."

Marcel squeezed her hand back, but didn't let go. If she only knew that there was something about her touch that made him want to offer her the world right now. "Just knowing you support me means everything to me." He lifted her hand and kissed the back of it.

The smile spreading across her face told him he'd won. He'd give anything to see that smile every day.

"Thank you," Crystal said.

Her smile encouraged him. He conceded the wait-until-later battle he inwardly fought. Marcel released her hand and drew her close to him. He pulled her lips between his, relishing in the softness and taste of strawberries and coffee. When she softened in his arms, he continued massaging her lips with his, this time until she was breathless.

Crystal broke the kiss.

"I haven't been able to stop thinking about you, Crys. Something is happening between us, and I want to explore it to see where it leads us."

She nodded, but didn't speak, her chest still heaving from their kiss. Not giving her a chance to catch her breath, he kissed her again. Every nerve in his body craved her and took pleasure in the fact that she shared his feelings. She didn't say it, but he felt it with every move of her lips.

When he gathered the will to end the kiss, he rested his forehead against hers and said, "I know there's a lot happening right now, but I want you to think about us officially dating."

Crystal put just enough space between them to where she could hold his gaze and he could feel her breath on his skin. "I feel the same. When I came to your campaign kickoff event, I thought I was imagining the chemistry between us. But it's real, and I'm kind of having a hard time dealing with it since we've been friends for so long."

Marcel massaged the side of her face. "And that's what makes us perfect for each other."

"You might be right."

Marcel pulled her close and placed one lingering peck on her lips, igniting every nerve in his body before gathering the strength to pull away and put space between them.

For the next couple of hours, they talked about the statement he'd give later that afternoon at the press conference. They didn't spend a lot of time on that topic, as the conversation veered toward more personal topics. One of the most promising things he'd learned was that she wasn't opposed to love and a committed relationship again. Most women in her shoes wouldn't have the same outlook on relationships, so for him, that was promising, especially since he'd just asked her to think about a future with him.

And the way her face lit up when she talked about her work at Langston Brands made his heart smile. He'd assumed that she transitioned in the role to get back on her feet after her disaster of a marriage to Dante, but it was work she loved. According to her, handbags were more than an accessory but part of a woman's wardrobe and style that made them feel good about themselves. And that was what she wanted to be part of—helping women feel good about themselves.

He enjoyed talking to her so much, it was hard to believe that four hours passed. Marcel tore himself away from her presence, dressed, and left the house to meet Olivia downtown on the steps of city hall for the press conference.

Thirty minutes, and this should be over so he could get back home to Crystal.

How good did that sound?

∞

Five minutes after Marcel left, Crystal changed her mind about staying behind. Being inside his house alone only exacerbated her fear. This person wouldn't win or force her to hide. She convinced herself that she'd be out in public so no one would try anything crazy.

It was because of her that Marcel was in this mess so Crystal needed to be there for him like he had been for her.

Crystal dressed in the first pair of wrinkle-free jeans she could find in her closet along with a black quarter-sleeve shirt and matching cargo jacket. She slipped into a pair of riding boots, draped her crossbody purse over body, scooped her car keys off the dresser, and headed to her car. She'd only be there for a few minutes. No drawing any unwanted attention to herself. No staying behind for questions and answers. In and out. Long enough for him to see her face.

Marcel thought it best that she park in his detached two-car garage. The second she stepped out into the cool afternoon air, an eerie feeling snaked up her spine. She charged it to the sudden change in temperature and trudged from the back door to the detached garage.

"Did you think I wouldn't find you here?"

Crystal jumped.

She dropped her keys, and her breath caught in her chest.

A disgusted, faint voice cut through the otherwise quiet walkway from the house to the garage. Her brain signaled her feet to run, but somehow they weren't getting the message.

"Didn't I tell you that you couldn't hide from me?"

The revulsion she held for her was evident in her eyes.

Crystal assessed the woman. About five inches taller than her and dressed in all black, her long hair tossed over her shoulders.

I can take her.

The woman must have read Crystal's thoughts because she advanced toward her in one fluid movement and shoved a gun into her side.

"You're coming with me. If you scream or draw any attention to us, you get a bullet to the gut."

∞

The news production team went through the motions of giving him a clip-on microphone and showing him where to stand on the steps. A crowd gathered around the area, murmuring and waiting for the conference to begin. He missed seeing Crystal's face among the crowd, but he knew why she couldn't be there. Marcel remained on high alert though, scanning the gathering of people for anyone suspicious—something hc wouldn't have been so cognizant of before, but recent events had him on edge.

Cameras flashed. Camcorders focused on him. The cameraman counted him down with his left hand. Five, four, three, two…

"A few weeks ago, I represented a long-time friend of mine, Crystal Langston, who was arrested and released from jail, in the murder of her ex-husband, NFL star Dante Green. As many of you are aware, my client was exonerated because she is innocent. Like you, I woke up to news this morning of an alleged conspiracy to commit murder. Crystal Langston nor myself are in any way involved in the murder of Mr. Dante Green. And frankly, I'm disheartened that someone would weaponize the events and use them against my campaign and our character."

Marcel moved away from his designated position and took a few steps to the left. "So, today, I reaffirm my commitment to ensure a criminal justice system that is fair, regardless of race, gender, and class, which focuses on solving serious crimes that harm our communities that are safe for the current and next generation. Questions?"

Marcel pointed toward a red-headed news reporter in the front of the crowd. She was poised with her voice recorder jutted in his direction.

"Attorney Singleton, do you think current DA Elliot Sanbridge is behind these alleged murder rumors to discredit you?"

He almost hoped it was him, but Marcel knew smear tactics were below Sanbridge. The man had always run a fair campaign. Instinct told him it was the same person behind the notes, but he couldn't dare bring that up.

"At this point, I'm not sure where the rumors came from, and I'd like to think that DA Sanbridge has no part in this."

She rattled off another question before he could move on to the next person. "Is this also the reason Ms. Langston is no longer the CEO of her family's company, Langston Brands?"

"I can't comment on Ms. Langston's role at Langston Brands. Thank you. Next question."

"The pictures of you and Ms. Langston in the headlines suggest you have an intimate relationship. Do you think your relationship with her has clouded your judgment?" he heard someone shout among the crowd, yet he ignored them and addressed another reporter at the opposite end of the front.

"Since your client's exoneration, do the police have any other suspects?"

"I'm not inclined to say. That's a question for the detectives working the case. My only concern is that my client doesn't serve time for a crime she didn't commit."

He shouldn't have been surprised at how many of the questions had to do with Crystal. At this point, no other arrests had been made for Dante's murder, so in the public's eye, she still looked guilty. After all, why wouldn't she want payback for Dante's physical abuse and public humiliation? But the world didn't know her like he did. If Crystal were to harm anyone, it would only be in self-defense.

The questions kept coming. Most of them the same, just worded differently. He finally gave the nod to Olivia, who sauntered from the sidelines to announce the conference was over.

"Attorney Singleton thanks you for your time and support of his grassroots campaign for district attorney. Have a good evening."

Marcel tugged the microphone off his shirt and handed it to the production leader. He and Olivia made strides toward his car. She wanted to talk business, but all he wanted to do was get back home to Crystal.

Olivia took two strides to match his one. "Hey, slow down. It feels like we're about to take off in a full-on sprint."

"Okay, but let's talk in the car."

There were eyes and ears everywhere, it seemed. After their five-minute walk to his car, he relaxed and gave Olivia his attention. He reminded himself not to worry about Crystal. She was safe—he'd made sure of it.

Twenty-One

Marcel dropped Olivia off at her car.

When she was safely inside and drove away, he called Crystal to let her know he'd finished and was on his way home.

Voicemail.

He tried several more times, but her phone didn't ring at all.

Worry clawed at his gut. Why would Crystal not answer her phone when she knew he was concerned about her safety?

Marcel swerved out of the parking area, breaking all traffic laws, except running red lights. Forget about being a courteous driver.

He kept calling her on the drive to his house.

Still no answer.

Twenty-five minutes later, which would have normally been a thirty-five-minute drive, Marcel swerved into his driveway. He climbed out of his car and raced to the front door. His fingers couldn't fly across the keypad fast enough to key in the unlock code.

"Crys," he screamed. He didn't want to scare her with his raised voice, especially if she'd fallen asleep, but worry squeezed his heart and lungs, making it harder for him to breathe.

No answer.

The house was empty and lonely.

Without searching through it, he knew it to be true. It was the same feeling that enveloped him every evening.

He rushed to her room, prepared to bang on the door, but the door was opened.

"Crys," he called to her again while he searched through the closet and en suite bathroom.

He ran out of the empty space, out of the house, and to the garage to see if her car was there.

When he made it outside, Marcel found her keys on the ground and her car parked in the garage. His body went numb.

Marcel whipped his phone from his pocket and dialed Layla.

When the line opened, he didn't think of pleasantries. Instead, he said, "Is Crystal with you?"

"No. I thought she was staying with you."

"Do you know if she had plans with your parents?"

"I doubt it. They're both here at the office. What's going on?" Her voice rose several octaves, fueling his own anxiety.

"She's not at my house and I found her keys in my driveway. Something isn't right. Send me a pin to her phone's location—now."

Marcel locked the door and ran back to his car. He thrummed his fingers on the steering wheel while he waited for Layla's message to come through. When it did, he put the info into his GPS and peeled out the driveway.

"Got it. I'm headed to look for her now. I'm twenty-seven minutes away."

"Marcel, now is a good time to tell me what's going on."

Marcel huffed. He didn't know what kind of danger Crystal might be in. She could very well be fine and this whole thing could be a misunderstanding. Though he had a feeling his optimism wouldn't serve him well in this situation. His instinct kicked in again. With her car parked in his garage and her keys on the ground, something was not right.

"Someone has been sending anonymous messages to her—not any direct threats of physical harm, but enough to have us worried."

"What? Why didn't you tell me—"

"It was Crys' choice. In case this turned sideways, she wanted to keep her family out of it."

"But—"

Marcel accelerated on the freeway around cars, which were moving a little too slow for him, even though they were traveling the posted speed limit.

"I understand, but she wanted to handle the situation herself. I've got this. I'll follow up once I confirm she's safe, okay?"

Layla was silent for at least fifteen seconds before she released a heavy sigh and agreed.

He wouldn't be surprised if she showed up to Crystal's phone location, and he wouldn't blame her.

Marcel dialed his office's private investigator, Naima.

"Tell me your investigation has turned up some kind of information that'll get me closer to finding out what's going on."

He tried to keep the panic out of his voice and suppress his concern for Crystal.

"Actually, I have. I was about to call you."

Oh no. What if Jacob abducted her or something crazy like that?

Marcel fought away such thoughts. He'd gotten bad vibes from Jacob, but so far, he'd determined Jacob's motivation to be money. Abducting Crystal just didn't make sense, but experience taught him that one never knew what a person was capable of when desperate or put in specific situations.

His heart adopted an erratic rhythm, so he let out a slow breath to focus on what Naima had to share.

"I managed to hack into his bank account and his computer. He's broke."

"What? How is that even possible?"

“Bad real estate deals and gambling. He’s up to his neck in a half million in debt. Three quarters of that he owes to loan sharks.”

“This is the information I need. Let me know if you dig up anything else.”

“Oh, but there’s more. The woman you mentioned as a possible associate, Wynter Washington, is having a house built in southwest Houston. Jacob lost money on his investment in that development.”

“Send me the address for that development.”

"Sending now. Oh, I haven’t found anything that links him to the messages Crystal received, but I’ll keep digging.”

“Thanks, Naima.”

Marcel’s thumb hovered over the button to end the call, but Naima called out to him before he pressed it.

“Oh, and Boss.”

“What’s that?”

“Whatever you do, be careful. Jacob Jackson is broke and desperate, and that makes him a dangerous man.”

But Marcel was even more dangerous when it came to protecting the woman he loved.

Loved?

Where did that even come from? He liked Crystal. Enjoyed her company. Wanted to explore his feelings, but not the L word, right?

Ten more minutes, and he'd arrive at his destination. Enough time to call Detective Diggins.

When the detective answered, Marcel didn't waste a second. "I think Crystal's been abducted." He explained his theory, including her parked car and keys on the ground. "Her sister sent me the location of her phone. I'm headed there now."

Marcel could hear the detective shuffling and his seat scratching against the floor. "Send it to me. Stand down, attorney. Let the police handle this."

Marcel ended the call.

Two minutes later, he turned into a new subdivision in Southwest Houston. After three turns, he pulled up to an unfinished two-story house. Three pallets of brick sat in the yard. The temporary door didn't have a knob, and the windows appeared to be newly installed. The protective covering hadn't been removed yet. The house was one of two on the street, in addition to a slab of concrete for the neighboring lots on either side of the house.

He texted the address to the detective, then, scanning the message Naima sent, Marcel noted it was the same address Crystal's phone location pinged from.

His stomach dipped.

Marcel climbed out of the car, taking in his surroundings. A large sign was out front. *Available.*

He took hesitant steps toward the plain wood entry door. Since there wasn't a doorknob, he pushed the door and stepped inside. The tile flooring was covered with brown paper littered with dusty footprints. He could see straight to the back door from the entrance.

His footsteps were light as he peeped around each door opening. When he made it to the stairs, he locked eyes with Crystal sitting in a folding chair in the center of the living room floor. Her eyes were red and watery. She gently shook her head, and before he could speak, he felt the barrel of a gun pressed into his back.

Twenty-Two

"You screwed up my life," Wynter snarled and waved the gun around.

Crystal wasn't sure Wynter would use it. She mentally ran through hypotheticals to jump out of that seat and take the gun from Wynter.

But now Jacob stood there with a gun pointed at Marcel's back.

What in the world is happening?

"What are you talking about?" Crystal spoke through gritted teeth.

All she had to do was keep Wynter talking. She'd watched enough movies to hope that someone would show up and save her.

She didn't have the luxury of swooning over the fact that Marcel came looking for her because he now had a gun pointed at him, too.

"You made me kill Dante."

Crystal's insides froze at the revelation. If Wynter had no qualms about killing Dante, surely she wouldn't have an issue shooting her.

"How is that my fault?"

Wynter had this far-off hateful gleam in her eyes. "The only reason he wanted to leave the NFL was to be with you. We were supposed to get married and live happily ever after, but he just couldn't seem to get over you."

Wynter emphasized *you* by shoving the gun at Crystal's chest.

Crystal thought her body would seize from the contact.

She turned her attention to Jacob. "And you're okay with this? Did you hear what she just said? She killed your best friend."

"But Wynter is my cousin, and you ruined both of our plans."

"I don't understand how any of this is my fault. I left Dante, remember?"

"Too bad it wasn't enough for him to move on with Wynter, marry her, and stay in the league just a little longer. Just a couple more seasons I told him." He scoffed. "But no, he wanted to chase you around Texas. All this BS about him wanting his wife back. He'd made his money, now it was time for him to do right by you."

Crystal locked gazes with Marcel. He was trying to think of a way out of this, too. She could see it in his eyes. Surely, she could take Wynter down, but Jacob was probably deranged enough to shoot her and Marcel.

"Dante knew I wasn't coming back to him. We've been divorced for over a year now."

"Silly woman. All of this is happening because of you. You think he would've stopped trying to get you back? You were just a trophy wife anyway. Never did him any good. If anything, being married to you held him back. He had much more potential than he realized."

"Jacob, I thought we were friends." Crystal couldn't believe Jacob thought of her that way, let alone had the nerve to say it. It was no secret that Jacob was obsessed with money, but now it was clear that money was all that mattered to him.

"Dante was my friend, too."

"And blood is thicker than water," Wynter interjected with that old cliché.

Wynter paced the area in front of Crystal, still waving the gun with every word she spoke. Disdain for Crystal spilled from her eyes and dripped with every word that came out of her mouth. "Our plan was perfect, wasn't it, cuz? We'd be living the high life. Shoot, I may have even had the chance to be on one of those reality shows like *Real Housewives.*"

"Killing him doesn't seem like the solution to your problems. You could've still married him."

Jacob jumped in, “Yeah, she could’ve, but as my top client, Dante being out of the game was an L for me. He owes me, but he left his entire estate to you. So now you owe me.”

“How do you know that?”

Jacob shrugged. “Harley and I go way back, plus, you’d be surprised at what a person would do if you toss a couple of bills their way.”

“Jacob, I don’t want anything to do with Dante’s estate, him, or you. For all I care, you can have it all.”

“Well, now that makes things easier for everyone involved, doesn’t it? But sweetheart, it doesn’t work that way.”

Since Jacob and Wynter were on a tell-all spree, she figured she’d try to get all of her questions answered. “So you are the one behind the text messages?”

“No, honey, that would be all me,” Wynter said, her chest puffed, like she was proud of herself.

“You two won’t get away with this, you know that, right?”

“Oh, but we already have. There’s no evidence of us being near Dante when he was killed. Plus, I was his agent and best friend. I have no motive in the cops’ mind. I should know, I’ve been keeping tabs on their li’l investigation, too.”

Crystal glanced at Marcel and saw something flash in his eyes. He knew something, and she wished he could share it with her right now. Because from where she sat, Jacob had a point. This would've been the perfect situation to wear a wire and have the cops waiting outside, poised to burst into the room at any moment now, but that was wishful thinking.

Crystal rewound the events of that evening trying to figure out how Jacob and Wynter managed to get away with murder. "I'm confused. Just how did you get in the room with Dante without anyone seeing you?"

"We were already inside," Wynter said. "When I left the stage, Jacob came to check on me. We'd been discussing our plan B when you and Dante came into the room."

"We heard the argument you and Dante were having, too. At that point, we knew what we had to do and were certain you'd take the blame for it. You telling him that you'd kill him was perfect," Jacob added. "I hate it had to come to that for my man, but sometimes in life we have to make tough choices."

It was as if she never knew him. What would make Jacob so desperate that he'd kill his best friend for money?

She nodded toward Marcel.

"So why bring my attorney in this?"

"Too nosey. Sniffing around where he doesn't belong. He should've walked away when he got you out of jail. Just couldn't leave well enough alone, could you, playboy? Love her too much? Is that it?"

Marcel didn't answer. Fire filled his eyes though, and she prayed someone intervened soon before he did something that could get them both killed.

"You don't have to answer. I remember how you pined over Crys back in college and how much of a punk you were when Dante told you to back up off her."

Jacob scoffed and sneered again.

Marcel lunged toward him, but Jacob lifted the Glock up to his forehead.

"Try it again, and you're as good as dead."

Unfazed, Jacob pulled out a folding chair that had been leaning against the wall. He slid it next to Crystal and said, "Sit down next to ya girl, partna. That way y'all can die together."

∞

Marcel was tired of this jerk.

His babble wasn't getting them anywhere.

Jacob was one-and-a-half his size, but Marcel perceived his own strength to be greater. Marcel worked through several scenarios in which he could overpower Jacob and take his gun, but none of them came without the risk of him or Crystal being shot by Wynter.

Perhaps if he and Crystal could both make their move at once, they had a chance of making it out of there alive and without anyone getting hurt.

As an attorney, he worked with Naima, their office investigator, from time to time to dig up facts to prove their clients' innocence, but he'd never been held at gunpoint. He made eye contact with Crystal, who'd been studying the situation herself. She'd told him about her self-defense classes and time at the gun range, but had any of that prepared her for what they were experiencing right now? His best guess was no, but regardless of the answer to that question, his primary goal was to protect her.

Marcel inserted himself into the conversation—well mostly monologue. "All Crystal needs to do is write a letter disclaiming the assets. She won't have any control over who gets it. You're wasting your time."

"You think I haven't done my research? I know all the little nuances. Crys here is going to accept everything and then hand it over to me, and you're gonna make sure she doesn't make any mistakes in the paperwork." Jacob shoved the gun against her temple. "Ain't that right, Crys?"

Marcel didn't have a weapon, but his voice was threatening, "Keep that gun out of her face."

Jacob pointed the weapon at Marcel's forehead. "Would you rather I put it in yours? There are enough bullets to go around for everyone."

"You better make sure you don't miss."

Jacob shoved the gun into Marcel's temple.

Marcel gritted his teeth. His body heated with anger. Beads of sweat gathered at the back of his neck. He didn't think Jacob would pull the trigger, not when it decreased his chances of getting away with this foolishness.

"This isn't a game, attorney, and one more comment like that just might earn you a spot next to my friend."

Jacob shoved Marcel's head with the gun before lowering the cool steel.

"This seems like a lot to go through. I don't understand why you didn't just talk to Crystal about this. She doesn't want Dante's estate. In fact, she would've been happy to transfer everything to you."

"Sounds easy enough, doesn't it? But we're past that point. Once I get everything I want, she has to die—and so do you."

Jacob grabbed a fistful of Crystal's hair and shoved the gun into her neck.

Wynter had become lackadaisical with the gun. She'd forgotten about her gun with it pointed in the direction away from Crystal and toward the wall. Marcel lunged toward her and wrestled it from her grasp and turned it on Jacob.

"Get your hands off her."

Twenty-Three

Where were the cops?

They should be here any moment now.

If Marcel and Crystal could hold Jacob and Wynter off a little longer, keep them talking, then he and Crystal could get out of this unscathed.

"You might as well lower that gun, playboy. We both know you won't use it. You've got way more to lose than I do."

"Yeah, because you've practically lost everything already with your bad real estate investments and the money you owe to loan sharks."

Surprise registered in Jacob's eyes.

"Somebody's been doing their homework. See, Wynter, I told you, too smart for his own good. Sticking his nose where it doesn't belong. So now you know why your girl here needs to sign everything over to me."

"It won't do you any good in jail," Marcel countered.

"Wynter and I will be long gone when your dead bodies are found."

Wynter kept her seat across from Crystal. She smirked and checked out her manicured nails. "That's right, cuz."

"I can't believe you're dumb enough to think you're not gonna pay for this," Crystal said.

Jacob pulled her hair tighter.

"Ouch."

"The only one who's gonna pay for anything is you."

Jacob nodded toward Wynter. She walked out of the room and returned with a notebook and pen, dropped the notebook in Crystal's lap, and shoved the pen into her hand. Wynter stood next to Jacob and peered over Crystal's shoulder. Jacob released her hair and shoved the gun in Crystal's direction. "Go on. Write the letter," Jacob said, snarling. "Keep it simple, and make it believable."

Marcel kept his gun aimed at Jacob. He watched Crystal write the disclaimer letter, rejecting Dante's assets, but Jacob wasn't as well versed in the law as he thought. Crystal would have to get the letter notarized.

The window to overtake Jacob narrowed. His mind raced with more scenarios of how he could knock the gun out of Jacob's hand. If he were to do that, Crystal would need to move fast to recover it and make sure Wynter was secured. Or he could grab Wynter and force Jacob to lower the gun away from Crystal. He was also close enough to grab Crystal and shove her behind him, protecting her from Jacob.

When Crystal finished writing, she slammed the notebook and pen on the floor and locked eyes with Marcel. He looked from her to Wynter, then back at Jacob, then gave a slight nod. Did she understand what was about to go down?

Jacob released her hair and knelt to picked up the notebook.

Marcel glanced at Crystal again. This time she gave a slight nod.

Crystal dove to the ground behind Wynter's chair.

Marcel slid his weapon across the floor to her and lunged toward Jacob to wrestle the gun out of his grasp.

Jacob squeezed the trigger and the bullet struck Wynter in her left arm before he dropped it.

"You shot me," Wynter screamed and clutched her arm.

Jacob shouted an expletive, but Marcel didn't care. He secured him in a chokehold. "I told you not to point that gun at her again," Marcel puffed out through heavy breaths.

Though Marcel didn't want anyone to get hurt, a wave of relief rushed through him when the bullet struck Wynter instead of Crystal. She'd dove to the ground at the perfect time.

Through ragged breaths, Jacob said, "How's it gonna look for Houston's future DA to have blood on his hands?"

Marcel tightened his hold.

"Why don't you let me worry about that?"

Marcel heard car doors slam and glanced toward the front door. Detective Diggins trailed four armed police officers running through the entrance.

Crystal knelt at Wynter's side. She'd removed her jacket and wrapped it around Wynter's arm to reduce blood loss.

The first officer pressed a button on the handheld radio positioned near his right shoulder. "We need an ambulance at 41652 Summer Cove Drive."

Jacob tried to wriggle out of Marcel's hold, but Marcel squeezed tighter. After framing Crystal for murder, sending the harassing notes, and the worry he'd caused him, Marcel wanted to snap Jacob's greedy neck.

Jacob squeezed out, "Ease up, bro. This has nothing to do with you."

"Oh, it has everything to do with me. The moment you decided to frame Crystal is when you made this about me. When anyone messes with the woman I love, they mess with me."

Love.

The word slipped out of his mouth, and he couldn't take it back. Was he just caught up in the moment? His adrenaline pumping. His emotions on high alert.

Crystal's head popped up.

She'd heard it, too.

He could see the questions in her eyes. No time to deal with that now, though.

"Attorney Singleton, we've got it from here," one of the officers said.

The officer placed Jacob's hands behind his back and tightened the handcuffs. He read Jacob his Miranda rights while he led him through the house back out of the front door. His partner accompanied them.

Minutes later, the ambulance arrived. The EMTs lifted Wynter onto the gurney. The third officer went with her and the EMT team. Marcel could hear the officer reading the Miranda rights to Wynter as well.

The fourth cop who identified himself as Officer Bailey took their statements while Detective Diggins stood and took his own notes. Crystal went first, detailing the events from the time Wynter pulled a gun on her and forced her to leave Marcel's house to the second the cops came inside. Marcel listened intently. He wanted to be upset that she chose to leave the house after they'd already agreed she'd stay.

Would this have happened if she never stepped outside the house?

Would Wynter have waited her out?

Was this encounter inevitable?

He'd been so focused on Jacob, he never stopped to think that Wynter could be involved. He could've had the security guard add her to the do-not-enter list as well.

But the other part of him found it admirable that she'd chosen not to become a prisoner to fear and that she wanted to show her support for him despite what was happening in her world.

After Crystal gave her statement, Marcel followed. His story corroborated hers, with the addition of his conversation with Naima.

Marcel, Crystal, Detective Diggins, and Officer Bailey walked out of the house.

Detective Diggins shook Marcel's hand. "Attorney, thank you for giving me a call. I'm glad the two of you weren't hurt." Then he shook Crystal's. "Even after you were exonerated, I still had my suspicions about you. Please accept my apology."

"You were just doing your job."

"And apparently, I'm getting a little rusty. Take care of yourself, Ms. Langston."

"Thank you for taking the matter seriously, detective. I appreciate your swift response to my call. We don't know how things would've turned out if you and your fellow officers didn't show up when you did."

"And good thing we don't have to find out."

Detective Diggins nodded and left the two of them standing in the driveway. The last officer followed him.

Marcel pulled Crystal into his arms and held her for a while, reveling in the fact that he'd found her, and despite that scene inside, she was okay. Her head rested against his chest. And now, just like it had for as long as he could remember, she felt like home.

Twenty-Four

"While I'm relieved you're alright, and I hate to break up this hug fest, you have some explaining to do," Layla said. She'd pulled up as Officer Bailey and Detective Diggins left.

Layla folded her arms across her chest and planted her feet. Crystal released Marcel and threw her arms around her sister. There was a moment inside that house where she thought Jacob or Wynter might shoot her. She was glad to be alive.

"I know, and I'm sorry I kept you out of the loop. We didn't know what was going on or the level of seriousness behind all this. My sole intent was to keep you guys safe and as far away from this mess as possible." Crystal released her. "You understand that, right?"

"No, I don't. This is insane, Crystal. You could've been killed today, and I would've blamed myself for not pushing harder and digging deeper to find out what was going on with you. And if

Marcel hadn't called me about tracking your phone, I wouldn't have known about this until it was much too late."

"I didn't want you to worry." Crystal released a heavy sigh. "I'm just glad it all worked out. I have you and Ava to thank, though. Joining that family tracking app was a good call. Probably saved my life today."

Layla's frown dissipated, seemingly satisfied with that fact. She playfully shoved Crystal's shoulder. "I guess. I may need to track your car and put a tracker under your skin, too, if you're gonna be involved in dangerous situations like this."

Crystal stepped closer to Marcel and exchanged glances with him. "Whoa, settle down. Lord knows I hope this is a one-off situation. I just happened to be connected to a crazy, greedy man. Thank God Jacob will get what's coming to him. Wynter, too."

Marcel turned her in his arms and pressed his lips against hers. "I was so worried about you. You don't know how happy I am you're alright."

"Thank you for coming to look for me."

"I couldn't see myself doing anything less for you."

"So are we just going to stand here and not address the fact that you two are kissing?"

Crystal chuckled. "What do you want me to say?"

"Are y'all an official thing or what?"

Crystal looked to Marcel before answering. “We haven’t gotten that far yet, but I’ll be sure to let you know when we decide.”

“From the looks of it, the decision has already been made.”

Layla hugged Crystal and Marcel. “I’m glad you guys are safe. And seeing as though Marcel’s got you covered, I’m gonna head out. Call me later.”

After Layla climbed into her car and left, Marcel led Crystal to the passenger side door and opened it. He rounded the car, took his seat behind the wheel, and shifted to face her.

“I guess this means you’ll be safe in your own home tonight.”

Earlier that morning, hesitation clawed at her when Marcel offered her one of his spare bedrooms as a haven. Now that she didn’t need it anymore, the thought of not having him near left a hollow feeling in her gut.

“Maybe, but just to be on the safe side, I’ll stay in your spare bedroom tonight.”

Twenty-Five

Freedom.

That word never sounded so good.

Even though she'd only served two days in jail, mentally and emotionally, she'd been locked up since this ordeal started about a month ago.

The storm was over now. Today, she lived in her rainbow.

Crystal strutted through the offices of Langston Brands to the Hobo conference room. She had so many reasons to be on cloud nine today. The nightmare of the past month was over. Her weekend getaway with Marcel. Reclaiming her seat as CEO of Langston Brands.

Crystal arrived first and stood in the doorway to the conference room. The aroma of fresh pastries and coffee filled the room, combined with the cashmere woods scent of the wall plug-in. Memories of her first day on the job flooded her mind. She was determined to get her life back after her divorce from Dante. Work and putting her business degree to use were first on her agenda. It had always been the plan for her to go to business school, return home, work at Langston Brands, and eventually become CEO.

After a year of throwing herself into her job, her father deemed her ready, and she'd taken the company to new heights in her short time as CEO. That Dante fiasco wouldn't stop her.

Crystal strode to her seat at the head of the table, ran her hands along the cool genuine leather, and sat. The cushion molded to her body.

This is how things are supposed to be.

Her phone vibrated in her hand. She flipped it over, hit the side key, and read the message.

I'm proud of you. Can't wait to see you tonight.

Crystal smiled at Marcel's message. Her sentiments mirrored his. Who would've thought her longtime friend would be the one who brought so much joy into her life?

Same here. Thank you.

"That's some kind of smile," Layla said when she walked into the conference room. She claimed the seat to Crystal's left.

"You'd be smiling, too, if you had the weekend I had."

Layla waved her hand. "Let me guess? Marcel?"

Crystal maintained her grin in response.

"Have y'all made it offi—"

Rick announced himself as he walked into the room. His presence shut Layla up.

"Welcome back," Rick said, though his voice was far from convincing.

"Thanks, Rick. I know you've done a great job in my absence. I'll have to take you out to lunch as my way of saying thanks."

Rick's lips curled into a smile that didn't quite reach his eyes. She and Rick worked well together for the most part. Crystal genuinely wanted them to have a better relationship despite the fact he couldn't remain acting CEO.

As if someone sounded an alarm, the remainder of the board filed into the room after Rick. Her father and mother sat next to Layla. Non-family board members sat to the right of Rick.

Her father opened the meeting. "First order of business is to reinstate Crystal Langston as CEO. All in favor, raise your hand."

All hands raised, except Rick.

"All opposed?"

Rick opposed the motion. Crystal was certain he still had his issues with her coming back, but thankfully, he didn't have the final say.

Lamont Langston scanned the room. "Then the motion is carried. Crystal Langston, you've been reinstated as Langston Brands' CEO."

Her father went on to thank Rick for serving in Crystal's capacity while she was away. Crystal's heart swelled from the approving eyes of her family. Distracted by her own thoughts, she missed whatever Rick said in response to her father's gratitude for his work. The board members applauded, and although Crystal had no idea why, she did the same.

"I think we're ready to discuss the launch event of our new bag collection," Crystal said. She picked up a tiny remote from the conference table and pressed a button. A projector screen rolled down, and the picture of their new handbag collection lit the screen.

Before she met with Marcel this evening, she had a press conference scheduled to address the events over the past month and to reaffirm her commitment to their brand and customers.

Everything in her world was now exactly as it should be.

∞

Life had been crazy over the past month.

But that craziness fed Marcel's campaign, and for that part of it, he could be thankful. It wasn't planned, but his role in solving the case highlighted his campaign goal of putting the right people behind bars. Donations from his grassroots campaign were rolling in. He wasn't sure if Olivia was happier than him the way she beamed when delivering the news.

Marcel purchased two dozen long-stemmed red roses. He left one dozen in a vase. He tore the petals off the other and sprinkled them on the new blanket he'd purchased for fireside meals with Crystal. He chilled a bottle of white wine in a bucket, which he set on the outer corner of the blanket. Marcel flipped the switch to turn on the fireplace and turned on the music. Brian McKnight's "Back at One" began to play through the Bluetooth speaker.

The doorbell rang. Takeout steak and shrimp with vegetables delivered. He tipped the deliveryman and placed the food containers on the countertop. Marcel flipped his wrist to check the time. Crystal should be arriving any minute now.

The doorbell chimed five minutes later. His heart thudded in his chest. Crazy how he was nervous today, after knowing her most of his life.

Marcel reached the door in four long strides, took a deep breath, and swung open the door. He drank in her beauty. Curls framed her face. She wore a little eye shadow, which made her eyes appear wider. Red lipstick framed her smile. He didn't know what kind of dress it was, but he didn't think she wore the sleeveless black dress to work that day. As chilly as it was this evening, he was surprised she didn't wear more than that little lace shawl over her shoulders. He glanced at the open-toed heels she wore. Her polish matched her lipstick.

He had to restrain himself from pulling her into his arms with the intention of getting her lipstick on his own lips.

"You look beautiful. Come on in."

"Looking handsome yourself."

After Crystal stepped inside and Marcel shut the door behind her, he couldn't help himself. He pulled her into a strong embrace and covered her lips with his. The softness of her felt like home.

Marcel released her, and Crystal rubbed the smudged lipstick from his lips. She turned to face his fireside setup and covered her mouth with her hand.

"Roses? This is so nice. Thank you."

His chest puffed. "Dinner is here, too. Steak and shrimp. I don't know how you feel about sitting in front of the fireplace with your dress on, but the area is ready, just in case," he quickly added. "I remember how much you like sitting there."

Crystal pressed a palm into his chest, and he thought he might melt from her touch. "You know that's my spot. Grab a pillow, and I'm all good."

Marcel rushed out of the room and returned with two pillows. He helped her to her space on the blanket and handed her the pillow for her lap. Once she settled, he grabbed the food from the counter, two wineglasses, and returned to claim his space in front of her. He blessed the food, but hesitated to take his first bite.

"You know, Crys, no doubt we want to put the past month behind us, but the time spent with you, no matter how insane, I don't want it to end."

Crystal's fork was half-raised to her lips. She lowered it and gave the kind of smile that made him believe—or at least hope—she felt the same, so he continued.

"You've been through a lot, but you should know I'm willing to wait until you're ready. Now that we've reconnected, I feel like we've been given an opportunity to do what we probably should've done years ago—date each other."

Crystal put her food to the side, pushed herself up onto her knees, and leaned in his direction. She cupped Marcel's face in her palms and smudged her lipstick on his lips again. The kiss was slow, deep, and intimate. His heart raced so fast, he was fairly sure a heart attack was imminent.

She pulled away and murmured against his lips. He could feel her breath on his skin. "I'd like that. In all this madness, you were the one who kept me sane."

Crystal didn't move from the position in front of him. He gazed into her eyes, unsure if he should express his emotions, or if his true feelings might push her away, but he chalked up his fear of the unknown. This was their second chance, and he'd promised himself if he ever got the opportunity, he'd be honest and not withhold any part of himself from her.

Marcel caressed her left cheek. "I love you, Crys. I think I always have, but at this point in my life, I know I always will."

"I love you, too, Marcel."

Most sane people would say they'd never want to experience the ordeal he had over the past month, but Marcel would do it again if it would bring him to this moment. His heart and home were now full.

THE END

Dear reader,

What did you think of Crystal and Marcel? If you've read any of my previous books, by now you know I'm a lover of second-chance romances. I just get all the feels when people (real or fictional) get to explore life with the person who makes their heart sing, especially when it didn't work out or they missed the opportunity the first go round.

Crystal survived her abusive marriage to Dante. I did my best to be sensitive to the topic, while also giving you a clear picture of what happened in their relationship. If you, or anyone you know, is involved in an abusive relationship, please get help by calling, 800-799-7233.

Romantic suspense is a new genre for me, so I really hope you enjoyed The Reunion. Book 2, tentatively titled, The Wrong Seat, is up next. It is Ava's story. We didn't get to see much of her this time because she was out of the country for work. She's on her way back home, and because this is a romantic suspense, returning home won't be without troubles. I can't wait for you to read that one either.

Please take a moment to let me know what you think by leaving a review on Amazon/Goodreads/Bookbub.

Until next time,

Natasha

About the Author

Natasha writes Christian fiction and devotionals. When she isn't reading or writing, she spends her time working out, swimming or watching movies with her family. She lives in the Houston metro area with her husband and three children.

Connect with Natasha online:

Bookbub @NatashaDFrazier
Instagram @author_natashafrazier
Twitter @author_natashaf
TikTok @author_natashafrazier
Facebook @craves.2012
Website: www.natashafrazier.com

Also by Natasha D. Frazier

Devotionals

The Life Your Spirit Craves

Not Without You

Not Without You Prayer Journal

The Life Your Spirit Craves for Mommies

Pursuit

Fiction

Love, Lies & Consequences

Through Thick & Thin: Love, Lies & Consequences Book 2

Shattered Vows: Love, Lies & Consequences Book 3

Out of the Shadows: Love, Lies & Consequences Book 4

Kairos: The Perfect Time for Love

Fate (The Perfect Time for Love series)

With Every Breath (The McCall Family Series, book 1)

With Every Step (The McCall Family Series, book 2)

With Every Moment (The McCall Family Series, book 3)

Non-Fiction

How Long Are You Going to Wait?

CPSIA information can be obtained
at www.ICGtesting.com
Printed in the USA
JSHW052301210922
30776JS00001B/2